shoot down the stars

KATRINA MARIE

This one is for the Dreamers. Y'all are the best.

COUPLES ARE SPINNING around the floor, celebrating the marriage of the girl I used to have a crush on in high school. She isn't the one capturing my attention, though. No, it's the girl I haven't seen in years.

Amelia, Tonya's cousin, used to spend the summers here when we were kids. She was so full of life, and always bouncing around like a damn cartoon princess. She saw the world through rose colored glasses while I saw it for the shit hole it actually is.

Something has changed, though. Her smile is forced when people talk to her. Her gaze barely moving from the floor unless someone is directly in front of her. I've wondered about Amelia since seeing her at the New Year's party at Tonya's. The weight of the world on her shoulders was evident then, but it's worse now. As if she's one straw from breaking into pieces.

I know that feeling all too well. Growing up the way I

have, it's hard not to be cynical. Seeing all of my friends coupling up and living their happily ever after's pushes me further toward the fringes. Maybe I can befriend Amelia and we can be in our own little world of misery.

Someone slaps me on the shoulder. "Dude, you should smile more." Marshall laughs from beside me. He's always so upbeat about life. I envy him. He's never had to struggle. At least, not the way I have. The only time I've seen him mope is when Bianca wouldn't answer his calls last year. Now that he has his tattooed vixen by his side, he walks around as if nothing could burst his happy little bubble. I wonder what it's like to be that excited.

I shoot him a wide grin. "Is this better?" My lips straighten out as the music changes to one of those line dance songs that are customary at weddings.

"That might be the fakest smile I've ever seen." Shaking his head, he directs his gaze to the group of girls dragging a protesting Tonya toward middle of the yard where everyone is dancing. "It's a time for celebration." Noticing my scowl, Marshall's brows pinch in worry. "You're not still harboring a crush on Tonya, are you? I thought you said you were over that when you got in that fight with Jake last summer."

"No, I'm not interested in her anymore," I roll my eyes. "I haven't been since before we graduated." Crossing my arms over my chest, I take in the scene. Christmas lights are strung throughout the trees and a couple of floodlights illuminate the yard. We're all dressed in our Sunday best after a last-minute hitch forced the wedding to be moved here. "I just don't want to be here."

"Being here is better than being at home," Marshall gives me a knowing glance. Yep, my home life sucks. This sucks just as much.

He's not going to leave me alone about this. He's determined to make everyone as deliriously happy as he is. "I'll try to have a good time." Bianca moving closer to us catches my eye. "I think your girl is looking for you."

"So she is." He turns until he's standing directly in front of me. "For real, Randall. Have a good time. Be happy for them." He doesn't wait for a response. Instead, he jogs toward Bianca and wraps his arm around her waist. Lifting her up, he twirls her around until her head falls back in laughter.

Jealousy swirls through my gut. I may be bitter about love and relationships, but I *want* that. I want someone that gets me on a deeper level than anyone else.

Amelia stands and my eyes focus on her once again. Sadness surrounds her and I want to know who put it there. Not knowing if I'll ever see her again, I take a step in her direction. Before I make it over to her, Tonya's hooked her arm around her and sweeping her off to the house.

My shoulders sag, and I turn toward the side gate, ready to leave the party. Passing by the windows, I can't help but glance at the two women standing there. Amelia's wrapped in Tonya's embrace. I want nothing more than to walk inside and comfort her. Something draws me to her, and I can't explain it.

Fighting the urge to open the door, I continue toward the gate knowing I'll never get the chance to know the girl who seems just as broken as I am.

ONE

amelia

A SOFT KNOCK on the door pulls my attention away from the crossword puzzle I'm playing on my phone. It's kicking my ass, though I'll never admit it. I've been living with Uncle Jason and Aunt Lucia for almost a month, and they still approach my room with caution. Well, it's actually Tonya's old room made evident by all the Bush posters hanging on the walls. Her obsession runs strong, and I don't blame Reaf for not wanting her to take the entire collection.

"Melly," my uncle's voice floats through the closed door. "Are you awake?" I cringe at my childhood nickname. It was my absolute favorite when I was younger. It made me feel special. I was also the only kid with a nickname. But now... Now it feels childish. As if I'm waiting for an adult to scoop me up in their arms and keep me safe. I don't correct him, though. He has to be missing Tonya now that she's on her own.

I've never heard my uncle sound as unsure of himself as he does right now. They act as if I'm a caged animal waiting to attack. Maybe I've given them reason to believe that. No, there's no maybe. My attitude hasn't exactly been the best, but I'm still adjusting. To be perfectly honest, I'm still hurting, too. They say not to run away from your problems, except I couldn't leave home fast enough. I need to reset my frame of mind if only to make things easier on my aunt and uncle.

"Yeah, I'm up." Living with morning people is something I don't think I will ever get used to. My feet drag as I walk toward the door causing my socks to get stuck awkwardly between my toes. If any movie needed zombies for extras, I'm certain I would fit right in. Messy hair, smeared mascara, and all.

I pull the door open, and I don't miss Uncle Jason's flinch. Or the small smile he's trying to hide. "Are you sure you're up? Because you could pass for one of the living dead."

And this is where I get my humor from. Even though I was a ray of sunshine when I was younger, I never hid my morbid sense of humor. "Funny, I was just thinking the same thing," I say around a yawn.

"You even sound like one," he laughs. "Get ready, kiddo. Lucia is almost done with breakfast."

"What," a smirk forms on my lips. "You don't like having zombies attend breakfast?"

He holds his hands up in surrender. "Hey, zombies

are welcome at my table any time. But... I think she's dropping you off at Tonya's when she goes to pick up Layla. She thinks you need to get out of the house more than you do now."

Groaning, I nod. "Why couldn't you be the one related to my mom? I feel like there would be less meddling if that were the case. I'd rather stay in bed and get some sleep. I can visit Tonya anytime. She lives less than ten minutes away."

"Not everyone has a cool uncle like me." He peers around the corner, making sure Lucia is nowhere in sight. "Look, I know things are rough for you right now. Hiding from the situation isn't going to make it any better. You need to get out and live your life. What people say about you doesn't matter." His voice is louder now. "Now, get ready before your aunt comes in here. She may be a softie most days, but she has no problems yanking the covers off of you. Just ask Tonya."

"I heard that," Lucia's voice is faint. How in the hell did she hear us from the kitchen? I've always said she has freaky super powers. I wonder if Tonya has them, too. Now that she's a mom and all.

"I'll be in there soon."

"You might have fifteen minutes before it's all ready."

So much for a long shower. "Okay, I'll hurry." And it's not a lie. I know how much of stickler my aunt is about time. She's always early to everything, and it just doesn't work well for me. I can count on one hand how many times I've been early for something. It's usually because I'm with Lucia. Otherwise, I'll get there when I get there.

All of my things are scattered around the room. Clearly, I haven't taken the time to put things away. If all goes well, I'll be here for a while. Even if it doesn't, I can't go back home. The rumors and mean girls are the reason I left that place. Tonya always complains about everyone here knowing everything. My town is even smaller, and most of the people there didn't bother coming to the source to find out what really happened. One misunderstanding led to my destruction, and I refuse to allow that to happen again. If that means I need to be a bitch, then so be it. Protecting my heart is more important than making friends any day.

Shuffling through the box on the bathroom counter, I catch a glimpse of myself in the mirror. Uncle Jason wasn't lying. I look like hell. Finally, my hand feels the plastic packaging of my makeup wipes. It takes a solid five minutes to get the mascara off. I'm not even sure why I wore it yesterday since I spent most of the day on the couch watching movies.

"Are you almost ready?" Lucia yells.

Inhale. Exhale. She's the most impatient person I know. Well, she is with me at least. I don't remember her being this hard on Tonya. Then again, my cousin got her shit together after she found out about Layla. Admiration doesn't even begin to describe what I feel for my cousin. She's working, going to school, and taking care of a family. And what am I doing? Spending my days binge watching movies and stuffing my face with food. I'm disgusted with myself. Comparing myself to her won't do me any favors, but I need to do *something*.

"Amelia?" My head snaps up at the sound of her voice. Aunt Lucia is leaning against my door, her brows pinched together. "Are you okay?"

"Yep," I pop the "p," hoping the extra emphasis will convince her that all is right in my world.

"Are you sure?" She stretches her hand out, and brings it back to her side at the last second.

"Just doing a little life evaluation." My mouth parts in a wide, completely fake, smile. Sniffing the air, I change the subject. "Is that bacon I smell?"

The corner of her mouth ticks up, but there's still worry hiding in the depths of her eyes. They shouldn't have to worry about me, and I feel horrible that it's come to this. Hopefully the distance between myself and home will help me heal, or at least forget.

Lucia throws her arm around my shoulder. "Yep. I made an entire package because I know how much you love it. Let's eat. Then we can go see the cutest baby to ever exist."

"I don't know about that. Layla's kind of a hot mess." That child gets into everything. She's obviously never heard the term, "curiosity killed the cat." I hope Tonya's ready because that girl is going to be a handful as a teenager.

"She's an adorable hot mess, though." The way her eyes light up when she talks about Layla is everything. It reminds me of the way our grandmother, Lala's, eyes would sparkle when we would go see her. Seeing the love and support my family has for each other is what is going to help me get through this rough patch.

* * *

"Who's the cutest little girl?" Lucia squeeze's Layla into her. Her voice is high pitched and on the verge of shrieking. Tonya winces at the sound. She has this thing against baby talk, and I *swear* my aunt does it on purpose to annoy her.

When the baby talk continues, Tonya's gaze on her mom darkens and her cheeks are rosy from anger. A laugh escapes my lips, no matter how hard I try to squelch it. "Shit," I mutter. Her focus on me is like a laser beam. I'm not the one talking to her kid like that.

"Is something funny?" She arches one eyebrow. And, damn, I wish I had that magical power. I attempt giving her the same look she's pinning me down with. I'm pretty sure I'm failing. It's her turn to laugh. Not some small giggle, but she's laughing so hard she has to grab her stomach. "Oh my gosh, what are you doing?" Tonya gasps between breaths.

"Uh," I glance around the room, confirming she's not talking to anyone else. "The same thing you are...*obviously*."

Another snicker falls from her mouth. "You didn't

quite hit the mark. You look like you're in pain or constipated."

"I do not look constipated." Do I? Gah, I hope I don't. Even though I'm with my family, it's still embarrassing.

"If only I would have pulled out my phone and gotten it on video." She shakes her head as if I'm a lost cause.

I'm glad she didn't. That would have mortified me to no end. Knowing her crazy ass, she would have sent it to all of her friends, and I would be the laughing stock... once again. That can't happen here. Especially, since I moved here to avoid that. To no longer be the butt end of jokes and bullies wanting nothing more than to tear me down.

Noticing my slumped shoulders, her laughters comes to an abrupt halt. "Is everything okay?"

Nodding, I grab a tissue from her coffee table. "Nothing is wrong, I just can't handle people thinking, and talking, smack about me. I thought I'd be okay with the comment, but not so much." I feel ridiculous for getting so emotional over her even suggesting taking video of me being silly. And honestly, six months ago, I wouldn't have. I would have laughed right along with her. The actions of a few stole that carefree joy away from me, and I hate that I've given them the power to do it.

Tonya taps me on the shoulder. "I'm sorry, I shouldn't have said that. It pisses me off what those girls, and that douchebag, did to you." Pulling me into her arms, she sighs. "I wish I could erase everything."

"I know." The words come out as a strangled whisper.

"Are they still being assholes?" She asks, softly.

"Tonya, language. You stay on everyone else's butts about it. You need to also," Lucia scolds while tickling Layla.

Tonya rolls her eyes. "I know that, Mom. It's why I whispered it."

"Well, it wasn't much of a whisper if I heard it," my aunt laughs. "Why don't the two of you go out and do something? I'll stay here and keep this one occupied."

Layla's giggles fill the room as she tries to say "stop" while being tickled.

"Are you sure?" Tonya never asks for help with Layla unless she has no other choice. I can only imagine how frustrating it is for those that want to keep her for no other reason than to spend time with her.

"I wouldn't have asked if I wasn't sure." She smiles at us. "I planned on stealing her away for the day anyway."

Grabbing Tonya's arm, I start pulling her toward the door. "We'll see you later." Don't get me wrong, I like living with my aunt and uncle, even if they *are* early birds, but I also need this time with my cousin. To be around someone my own age.

"You know I need to grab my purse and keys, right?" Tonya slips from my grip right before I put on my hand on the doorknob. "I'll text Reaf and let him know you're here so he isn't surprised when he comes home."

Her mom snorts, "What? Does he come home ripping off his clothes for you?"

My cousin's cheeks turn bright red. "No," she shrieks. "Why would he do that?"

"He totally does," I yell, laughing. "Oh my God. I'm not ever coming over without calling beforehand again. That's definitely an image I don't want in my brain."

"Shut up," she swats my arm. "Let's go before Mom makes this whole conversation unbearable."

"Too late," Aunt Lucia sing-songs. "Y'all go have fun. And warn Reaf that I'm here. Because as much as love him as a son-in-law, there are things a parent should never have to see."

Tonya buries her face in her hands, and propels me toward the door. "Let's get out of here."

"Just a few seconds ago you were dragging your feet," I tease.

"My mom wasn't embarrassing the hell out of me a few seconds ago." She practically runs down the stairs from her apartment to her car, and I have to jog to keep up.

When Aunt Lucia told us to go out for the day, I assumed we would be going to the mall or out to eat. I didn't think we would end up at a hardware store of all places.

"Why are we here, again?" Whining isn't cute, I know that. At the same time, this isn't exactly my happy place.

"Because," she pauses while double checking the measurements Reaf sent her. "My *husband* wants to build me a shelf for all of my nerdy *Harry Potter* and *Buffy* things. Who am I to argue with that?" I think she just likes saying the word "husband."

Waving my hand toward the various sizes of wood, I huff. "But, why can't he get it?"

"He's at work, and we're out and about." She doesn't add anything else, as if that explains it all. And, I guess it does. I just don't want to be here. How are we supposed to have girl talk in the middle of *this* store?

Tonya reaches for a piece of wood, that isn't on top, and begins pulling it out. She doesn't see the box of open screws on top until it's too late. They tumble all over the floor at our feet, and her entire face turns pink. "Oh shit," she mutters.

A guy around our age turns the corner, no doubt to see what the noise is. An angry scowl marring his handsome face. He groans when he realizes what's happened. "Really, Tonya? I was about to take my lunch break."

"Sorry, Randall," she squeaks.

Randall... This is the kid we all used to play with when we were kids. I vaguely remember seeing him at the party but I was so tuned into my own misery that I can't recall actually talking to him.

For a split second his eyes meet mine. My. Heart. Stops. No, my heart can't react to this guy I no longer know. I will not let another person have a chance to break me wide open again. For the tiniest moment, the frustration leaves his face. It doesn't last long before he bends down to clean up the mess my cousin has inadvertently made.

randall

TODAY WAS ONLY another shit day until I heard something fall and hit the floor. Even if picking up Tonya's mess means I can't take my lunch break yet, it's worth it. It's worth everything to catch a glimpse of *her*.

I thought Amelia had gone back home after the wedding. Since Jake and Tonya broke up almost two years ago, I don't make it a point to hang out with her or her friends very often. The only time it happens is when Jake begs me to come along. It's a weird dynamic, their friendship. I applaud them for making an effort. For letting Layla know that she is loved by both of them, and so many more people. All kids deserve that, even if I never received the same treatment.

"I'm so sorry, Randall," Tonya says from behind me. "I didn't know there was something on top of the stack."

"This is why Reaf should have gotten the stuff for your shelf," Amelia mock whispers. She's purposefully being loud, and I can't stop the grin from creeping onto my lips. "You probably should have also grabbed the top board. Then you would have seen the screws."

"Shut up, *Melly*." She sticks her tongue out at her cousin. Melly? The tinge of pink gracing Amelia's cheeks tells me she doesn't like it.

"Would you stop calling me that?" Amelia hisses.

I think I need to stop this argument before they start wrestling in the middle of the aisle. Though, I doubt they still do that. I don't want to take any chances. Standing up, I hold out my hand. "Where's the list Reaf sent you? I can pull whatever you need."

She places the phone in my hand. "Here you go."

Glancing over the list, I shake my head. "This isn't even the right type of wood, Tonya."

She shrugs, not at all embarrassed. "How was I supposed to know? I looked at the sizes and they matched. What else is there to know?"

"A lot," I laugh. "This isn't even the section you want. The boards he wants to use are in the shelving area."

She twirls her finger in the air. "Lead the way, Captain Know It All."

"It's kind of my job to know these things." Amelia is standing off to the side now. She's looking at me, but trying to make it look like she's not. It's adorable. I stick out my hand in her direction after handing Tonya her phone. "I'm not sure if you remember me, I'm Randall."

"I remember you," she squeaks. She clears her throat and shoves her hands in the back pockets of her shorts.

"We used to get into all sorts of trouble when we were kids. How have you been?"

"Okay, I guess." Her asking how I've been wasn't what I expected. Hell, I can't believe she actually remembers me. "Nothing exciting. Work, work, and oh, more work. How have you been?"

"I'm okay, right now." Amelia's shoulders hitch up the slightest bit, trying to downplay the last part of her answer. I know that feeling. We find our happiness in moments of "right now."

Tonya claps her hands together. "Should we go find the shelving?" She eyes me as I turn toward her. Her glare is never a good thing. I used to laugh when she would direct it toward Jake. I'm not laughing now. That look is scary, and I can only imagine what she might have to say to me.

"Yeah, they are a few aisles down." The walk to the correct area is quiet. Conversations of other customers float through the air, but do nothing to calm my racing heart. Amelia remembers me. And she's *here*. I only need to find out for how long. Is it another short visit or is she living here? Obviously, I can't ask her because it'd be weird. Looks like I need to give Jake a call. Or, maybe Marshall. He wouldn't judge me for asking. Jake would ask me a million questions and let my interest slip the next time he talks to Tonya. I'm definitely talking to Marshall.

The shelves are on the bottom of the rack. Dusty from sitting for so long. "Here they are. We have them in a few different colors," I point to the three stacks. "Do you have a preference?"

She's still staring at me with pinched brows. "I like the black ones. We also need brackets." She turns toward Amelia, "Can you go grab those? I saw them one or two aisles over."

"I guess," Amelia answers. "How many do I need to get?"

Before Tonya has a chance to look at her phone, I answer. "I would get at least twenty. If that's too many, y'all can always bring them back."

"Okay," she drawls. "I guess I'll be right back."

The second Amelia leaves the aisle, Tonya turns on me. "What game are you trying to play?"

"What?" My head snaps back, surprised at her question.

"With my cousin," her arms cross against her chest. "Why do you have that spark in your eye? Like you want to get to know her better?"

Shit, she knows. What do I even say to that? "I'm not sure what you mean. We all grew up together as kids. It was just a friendly conversation."

"You are so full of crap. You can't hide the way you've been looking at her." Her voice rises, and she reins it into an angry whisper. "I'm not trying to be a bitch. Amelia has had a shitty few months. I will not let you damage her even more. Not after the bullshit she's gone through."

"Don't pretend to know a damn thing about me,

Tonya." I'm seething. "You haven't seen the shit I go through on a daily basis. All you see is the asshole facade I put on when I'm around everyone else."

She winces. "Look, I'm just trying to look out for my cousin."

Amelia rounds the corner. Arms full of brackets that are about to fall and confusion all over her face.

"Is that all you need?" I ask, bluntly.

Tonya only nods, regret in her eyes but not backing down from her need to protect her cousin from big bad me. "If you need anything else, you know where to look now."

Turning, I almost run to get away from them. There's no goodbye wave, or "nice to see you again." Just me... putting as much distance between myself, Tonya, and the girl I want to befriend. That did not go at all the way I had envisioned.

Leaving and taking my frustration out with a brisk run would help. Except I only have a thirty minute break, and rent is due next week. I need the hours. The break room is empty, and I run my hands over my face as I sit down. As I try to figure out what my next step will be, my lunch sits in my locker, completely forgotten.

Sadly, my day didn't get much better. Customers came in complaining about us not having the same exact thing other stores have. It took everything in my power not to scream. If they wanted the stupid flooring the other store had, they should have gone there to begin with. Dealing with pain in the ass people is the last thing I want to do after my confrontation with Tonya earlier.

"Randall," Tony, my boss calls out to me. "You can go ahead and head home."

"My shift isn't up, yet," I argue. Damn it. He can't send me home yet, I need a full week. Especially, if I still want a place to live. My piece of shit dad isn't going to get off his ass to help.

"Don't worry about it. I'll still pay you for the rest of your time." He looks at me knowingly. Stupid ass small towns where everyone knows my business. If I had been able to stay in school, I'd have left this shithole behind. "And," he continues, "that scowl on your face is scaring away the customers. Go get your head on straight and be ready first thing in the morning." With a gentle pat on the back, he walks away.

There are two options... I can go home and listen to my dad bitch about how worthless I am, or I can go to Marshall's. The choice is simple, really. Dad's harsh words can wait, I need to figure out what I'm going to do about Amelia, now that I know she's in town for a while.

Disturbed blares through the speakers. The perfect soundtrack to this crappy day. There's nothing like heavy rock to ease my mind.

I start in the direction of Marshall's parents when I remember that he got his own place. It's a habit to go to his parents' house. They feed me. It's not the only reason I liked going over there. It just happened to be the place where we all congregated when we wanted to hang out. Marshall's parents were the most welcoming, and weren't put off by having a bunch of teenage boys always at their house.

There's no way in hell I would want my friends to hang out with me at my house. Not because I'm ashamed of where I live, but because my dad is a raging asshole on the best of days. Nobody wanted to go to Jake's house either. They would have flipped their shit if we got one speck of dirt anywhere in their immaculate house. The few times we were over there, it was so awkward that we left as soon as we could.

When Jake told off his parents last summer, essentially cutting himself off from their funds, I couldn't have been prouder of him. Even if the main reason he did it was because of a girl. I mean, he also did it for his daughter because his parents were trying to do some shady shit. I think wanting to prove himself to Charleigh helped him come to the decision faster. If only I could do the same thing with my dad.

Once upon a time, I had a set of parents that were great and I felt loved. But Mom leaving and telling us she didn't want a family anymore destroyed the both of us. Dad stopped caring and started drinking. And that turned into yelling and getting physical when I did something he didn't approve of. That's a lot to deal with on top of changing hormones when you're a pre-teen.

And now, even though I'm twenty, I continue to let him treat me like shit. Instead of turning around to go to Marshall's, I make a U-turn and head home. As much as I want to get to know Amelia, I can't. She needs a friend who isn't broken, and who's not afraid to be left behind.

As much as I'm dreading whatever my father has to throw at me for being home early, it's better than the possible rejection I face after Tonya tells Amelia how much of an asshole I can be. Being thrown away for something shiny isn't a feeling I want to endure ever again.

amelia

"WHAT WERE you talking to Randall about?" We're sitting at a table in the food court of the mall. It seemed weird that she sent me off to get brackets on my own. A part of me wanted to walk to the next aisle and listen in on their conversation, but I decided that whatever it was probably wasn't any of my business.

"Nothing," Tonya replies, too quickly. She shoves a piece of pretzel into her mouth when she sees me eyeing her over my soda, knowing I'm not going to give this up.

"It didn't seem like nothing when I came around the corner." Placing the straw to my lips, I take two big sips. "I thought you all got along after you worked the co-parenting thing out with Jake."

After she swallows the huge piece of food in her mouth, she groans. "We do. I was just... warning him away from you."

"What gave you any indication that he was interested in me? I haven't talked to him in years. Literally." Am I so broken she thinks I'll latch onto the first guy that I see? I'm in no place for a relationship. After my ex made a spectacle of me in front of half the town, I don't need to be in a relationship. I'm still licking my wounds.

Hell, they ran me out of town from embarrassment. There's no way in hell I'm going to let anyone get that close to me again. I don't care how good looking they are. Or, if I can see the pain they carry with them. And let's face it, Randall has it hidden within the depths of him. I saw it in the frustration he showed at the spilled screws.

"You didn't see the way he was looking at you," my cousin argues. "It was like he was stranded in the desert and you were the water that would keep him alive."

"Whatever," I mumble. Happy that she didn't see my face when our eyes met for that split second. Even if I've sworn off guys, I can't help this need to get to know him better. Not because I think I can *fix* him, but because maybe we can help each other out of the darkness we are both stuck in. If he feels as alone as I do, he could use a friend.

I know I can hang out with Tonya, and her friends, whenever I want. They'd be happy to have me around. They are all coupled up, though and have a history together that I simply don't. The few times I've been around the entire group, I've felt like the spare wheel. Just along for the ride. Sometimes I'm the loneliest when I'm surrounded by people.

So wrapped up in my thoughts, I don't notice Tonya's

hand on my arm. The sounds of other shoppers talking, and their bags rustling, comes into focus when Tonya speaks. "I'm sorry, Amelia. I didn't mean anything by it. I just didn't think you would want to deal with guys, or their drama. And Randall... He comes with a lot of drama."

"That's for me to figure out," I sigh. "I'm not saying I want to date him, or anything. What could be so wrong with being his friend. He looks like he could use one."

"You're probably right," she finally agrees. "I don't think anyone is hanging out with him the way they were before. Jake is completely wrapped up in Charleigh, and doing everything he can to be a good father for Layla. Marshall's so focused on Bianca, it's sickening."

"I thought there was another kid we used to play with when we were little." My nose scrunches up at my own use of the word "kid." We're no longer children playing in the dirt. Some of us are on the cusp of twenty, or have already left our teen years behind. It feels silly using those words to describe us now.

Tapping her finger on her chin, she nods. "There was. His name is Dylan but he kind of bailed on everyone here at the end of last summer." She glances around as if she's deep in thought. "I think Marshall has reached out to him a few times, and never got a response." Another bite of pretzel and a shrug. "I'm not really sure what happened since they all stopped talking to me after I broke things off with Jake. Well, except for Marshall. He's always there for everyone. I do know that Randall can't rely on Dylan anymore. Not now that he's forgotten anyone here exists."

I consider asking her why he doesn't hang out with the friends he still has. But I know his reasons. I've felt them. As much as people want to include you in things, the exclusion is apparent. It's difficult being part of a group when they all have someone they can lean on, and you're off to side not knowing what to do.

"Let's go shop and find some things to decorate my new shelf." Tonya scoots her chair back and stands.

"Don't you already have figurines?"

"Yep, but it doesn't hurt to get a few more." She grabs her trash before turning. "Are you coming?"

"Sure," I exhale. "Only on one condition."

"What's that?" Adjusting the strap of her purse to keep it from falling off her shoulder. Her foot begins to tap. Patience is something my cousin has never possessed.

"You stop intervening on my behalf. I'm a big girl, and I can handle things myself." My butt is not going to leave this chair until she agrees. As much as I love her thoughtfulness, it drives me to my breaking point when she tries to do what she thinks is best for everyone else.

A pained look crosses her face, knowing she's thinking about all the drama I've already been through. "Deal." She waves me toward her. "Maybe we can also find some stuff to make the room at my mom's house truly yours."

Decorating my room hasn't been at the top of my to

do list. Nothing has really. Maybe adding my own touch will help me feel more at home. I wish I would have brought some of my things from home. Doing that would have brought reminders, though. It's time for me to make a change, and this is the first step toward doing just that. "Let's do this."

"That's more like it." She hooks her arm through mine, pulling me to the escalator. "You'll have a whole new room before we leave today."

If only fixing the heartache inside was as easy as plastering new posters on it.

* * *

"How was your day out?" Aunt Lucia calls from the kitchen. A spicy aroma fills Tonya's apartment and my mouth begins watering. It appears she's taken over Tonya's kitchen. It's a good thing, though. My cousin can't cook for the life of her. The only thing she's made since I've been here that's edible is macaroni and cheese.

"Good," I reply. "How did you even know we were back?" I set my bags beside the door while Tonya wanders off to find Reaf. Grabbing my new blanket from one of the bags, I walk to couch before collapsing onto it. Who knew shopping could be so tiring? Part of me wonders if it's because of who I was with. I've never been a huge shopper. Going in for what I want and getting out as quickly as possible. But Tonya... She has to look at every single thing. We could have been home over an hour ago.

"The door isn't exactly silent when you open it." She walks out of the tiny kitchen. "Tonya really should talk to the office about that so they can get maintenance up here. Anyway, I also heard the bags rustling." A dish towel is tucked into her jeans pocket when she sits down beside me. "I knew as soon as I heard them that Tonya had a successful shopping day. Did you get anything?"

"Yeah," I say through a yawn. "I picked up a few things for my room. Tonya kind of forced me to do it so I could make the space my own." Even though it's not permanent. It's something I have to keep reminding myself of. No matter what happens, I won't be here forever. I still have my own family back at home. My *friends* and ex-boyfriend are the only reason I need space from my home town. At least I thought they were my friends.

"Good," Lucia pats my knee. She must see through my thoughts because she adds, "You know you can stay as long as you want, right? There's no time limit. You are always welcome."

"I know," I mutter, burrowing myself deeper into my blanket cocoon. Out of all of my family, Lucia has always been my favorite. She's the most kind-hearted person I know, and willing to do anything for anybody. My mom tried to help me the best way she could when all the drama started, and we both agreed that getting away from the rumors and lies for a bit was best all the way around. It would give me time to get over the fact that my friends were all backstabbing assholes.

What did I expect, though? I went from being a loner to having one of the hottest guys in town interested in me. I should have known things were going to go badly when I was accepted into his group so easily. They weren't nice people when we were in school. It was too much to hope that maybe, just maybe, they had changed in between the short year since we graduated. But nope, some people never do. They continue to relish their asshole ways and torment whoever they see fit.

"Hey, Amelia," Reaf's voice booms as he comes into the room. Not expecting him, I jump. How in the hell does he walk so silently? I'm used to Tonya stomping around everywhere. You can hear her coming from a mile away.

"Hey." My voice is muffled from beneath my blanket. Sleep would come so easily nestled in here. I'm not sure what time Lucia plans on leaving, and a nap sounds amazing. Falling into a dreamless state would free my mind from the drama I'm attempting to run away from, and the thoughts of Randall that keep popping up. It's not a good idea. He's broken. I'm broken. What would a friendship between us accomplish? Shared loneliness is the only thing I can think of.

"I'm going to go finish cooking." Lucia's absence makes me feel like a small child wanting someone to make everything better. "We all know these three need something good to eat besides whatever Tonya's been feeding them."

Reaf fills her space. Not sitting too closely, but close enough that I can feel the small dip in the couch. "Hey, I'm the one that does most of the cooking," he protests.

As soon as the sounds of pots and pans moving around fills the silence, he shifts his body. Most likely until his back is against the arm rest. "What's wrong?" He pokes the blanket pile I'm under until he finally hits my shoulder. "And don't tell me nothing. It doesn't work with your cousin, and it's not going to work with you."

"Will not answering work?" Gah, his do-gooder self is so annoying sometimes. Always trying to make everything better. I'm surprised he and Marshall haven't formed some sort of "Make Everyone Happy" alliance. They would go around in capes, solving all the issues, one person at a time.

"Not even a little bit." He voice softens. "Really, what's wrong?"

"Where's Tonya?" If anyone can get me out of having to talk about my feelings, it's her. Or maybe Cami, but she's off at school and living her life with Travis. Ugh, all these couples make me cringe. I used to be ridiculously in love with the perfect boyfriend. Or, at least I thought I was, until he ruined that in one swoop.

"Putting up all the crap she bought. Thankfully, most of it was stuff for Layla. She needed some clothes for the summer. She's growing so quickly, we can't keep up." I feel his hand moving somewhere near my head. He grabs the edge of the blanket and pulls it down until my face is uncovered. "How do you even breathe with all of this on top of you?"

"I have a little space uncovered on this side to keep the air flowing." I point to the side opposite of him even though he can't see what I'm doing.

"I see," he nods his head "Nice try on the subject change, by the way. Tonya isn't going to swoop in here and rescue you." Pausing, he waits for me to respond. When I don't, he continues, "You can talk to me, you know that right? I won't say anything to Lucia and it won't get back to your mom. Keeping everything bottled up is only going to hurt you in the long run. I know, I've been there."

"You have?" That strikes me as odd. He's always so happy and chipper. It seemed like nothing ruffled his feathers.

"Yeah," he nods. "When my dad bailed on us. Bryce was just a baby, and I was so angry at the world. I acted out and made my mom's life a living hell for a while. In the end, it was for the best. Mom is living a better life without him dragging her down."

"Wow, I'm sorry. I didn't know all that." Gratitude that my parents are still together and in love, flows through me. "I knew he wasn't around but I didn't know he abandoned y'all."

"Don't get me wrong, we still talked on birthdays and holidays. He's just never gone the extra mile. It's one of the reasons I didn't invite him to the wedding. Why should he get to celebrate the greatest day of my life when he was around for so little of it?"

"It makes sense." I swear my cousin's husband is an old soul. He's so mature about life events. I guess he'd have to be when the person you look up to drops the ball.

"So, what's bugging you, cuz." And then he ruins the maturity by calling me "cuz."

Pulling my arms out from under my blanket, I throw them up in the air. "Everything."

Reaf raises an eyebrow waiting for me to continue, and I word vomit all over the place. "The guy I thought I was in love with shattered my heart into tiny slivers. And, as much as I try to fit in with everyone here, I can't help but feel like I'm on the outside because all of you have somebody to turn to. On top of that, we saw Randall at the hardware store today. I hadn't seen him since we were kids, only when our eyes met... It was like sparks flooded my nervous system. I can't be any sort of interested in anyone right now. I'm not over the bullshit I went through last year."

Brows furrowed he nods. Dear God, he looks like a freaking shrink. He may have gone into the wrong major in school because he's shockingly easy to talk to. At the same time, I feel like he's psychoanalyzing me. Ugh, how did my life become this feeling of constant dread and jealousy? I used to be happy, like Reaf. Now... Now, I have to force myself to smile so people won't constantly ask me what's wrong.

"First," he holds up one finger. "You always have

someone to turn to. We are here for you no matter what. If we're being super annoying with our coupledom, tell us to take it down a notch. Second," another finger goes up. "I don't know Randall that well. He's come to a few get-togethers at your aunt and uncle's house, and he usually stays to himself. He seems a little standoffish." Reaf takes a big breath. "And, lastly, what happened back at home? I asked Tonya but she said it wasn't her story to tell."

That right there is why she's my favorite cousin. I've always been able to go to her about what's bothering me. Until now. She knows because I've told her. It's just that I feel like my problems are miniscule compared to what she's trying to accomplish while also having a family.

Shrugging, I look toward the ceiling. "I got my heart broken."

"What did he do?"

The only place to start is the beginning. "I've always been kind of a loner. Doing my own thing and not really caring about anyone else. I didn't have any close friends when I was in high school. That didn't change when I graduated." Most people also wagged their fingers at me when I didn't go to college, too. I was happy working at one of the boutiques in town. It was where I thrived.

"When everyone came home for summer break," I continue. "The guy I had a crush on started coming into the stored I worked at. I didn't think anything of it. He was getting stuff for his sister, or his mom would send him in to pick something out for a gift for someone. At least that's what he told me." Deep breath in, exhale out. Even talking about it makes the wound bleed all over again. "One day he asked me out on a date, and instead of playing hard to get because I knew it was too good to be true, I said yes. We dated all summer, and kept it up when he went to school. Everything was fine and dandy. I got along with his friends, and they accepted me. At least for a little while."

"Until," Reaf swirls his hand wanting me to finish my story.

"Until it wasn't," I sigh. "It seemed like everything was going great. I was looking forward to Christmas break when he would be home again, and we could spend actual time together instead of over video. Instead, he ignored me for a couple of days after he got back. Then I saw that someone tagged him when I was scrolling through social media. It was a girl sitting in his lap at his parent's house. Of course, I went to his house right after that to confront him. He told me she was just a friend and didn't have anyone to go home to for the holidays so he invited her to his house.

"And you know what?" It's rhetorical, but I feel the need to say it anyway. "My dumb ass believed him. I'd never really dated before, and I didn't know what else to do. In my family, people don't lie to those they consider their own. When his friends started sending me pictures of the two of them together throughout most of the semester, I felt like an idiot. I confronted him and broke it off. That's when things went downhill."

Choking back a sob, I try to rein in my emotions. I can feel warm wetness sliding down my cheeks, and I hate that I'm still allowing this shit to bother me. "His friends started posting pictures of me on social media calling me a 'fat ass' because I'm obviously not really thin. And he started spreading rumors about me sleeping around. And how dare I break up with him for doing the same thing he was doing."

Another deep breath fills my lungs. "It was finally time for him and his friends to go back to school, and I thought it would end. He had the audacity to come to my house and tell me I was being ridiculous. 'How could you expect someone like me to stay faithful to someone like you when there are so many people out there?' Those were his exact words. He left, and people would give me the cold shoulder when they came into the boutique and the whispers never died. I was hurt and reeling from the blow he dealt me."

"Nobody should ever treat someone like that," Reaf shouts. "I don't care how highly they think of themselves."

"I found out after they left, that him dating me was some sort of joke. They wanted to see if they could get the class recluse to fall for him. I was already in a deep dark depression by that point. I didn't want to leave the house. My self-worth plummeted." I look up and see the rage on Reaf's face. Shocked that anyone would be such an asshole. "Mom and I decided it was best if I came here. Around people that could put me back together again. Family that could remind me what it's like to be truly loved and accepted."

"What college is he going to? I can always drive up and defend your honor." He's smiling but I know he's dead serious. This is what family does for each other.

Wiping the tears off my face, I snort. Leave it to my new cousin-in-law to make me laugh when I'm feeling down on myself. "He doesn't matter anymore." In all reality, he shouldn't. His words shouldn't still have an effect on me, except they do. I'm still trying to puzzle out what he meant by 'someone like you,' Is it because I'm not skinny? Or, because I lived my life as an outcast? I'll never know because I refuse to speak to him ever again. Even when I go back home.

Reaf taps me on the forehead, making me go cross-eyed for second focusing on his finger. "Chin up butter-cup. Leave the assholes behind and live the life you want to live."

"Athole," a small voice says from the doorway.

"Oh crap, I didn't realize Layla was standing there. Tonya is going to kill me." He rushes to pick up the girl that's become the center of everyone's world. "Of all the words to repeat, you pick that one?"

I burst into laughter. Holding my belly because if Tonya would have heard her daughter cussing, she'd be livid. Just then she enters the living room. "It smells amazing in here. I can't wait to eat whatever Mom is cooking up." She looks between me and her husband, noticing the laughs I'm trying to contain, and Reaf's deer in the headlight's expression. "What's going on?"

"Nothing," we say in unison. A giggle escapes me, and her brows pinch in frustration.

We're saved from her questioning because right at that moment Lucia yells, "Food's ready. Come eat." And if I know anything about my cousin it's that she lives for her mom's cooking.

Throwing the blanket off of me, I stand, feeling lighter. Like a boulder has been lifted off my shoulder. Reaf should definitely switch majors. He's missing his true calling.

randall

"STUPID, PIECE OF SHIT CAR." I kick the tire, wincing at the pain now shooting through my foot. This is just what I need. Another thing to add onto a day that has gone horribly wrong already. It's not even nine and I can count on one hand all the things that have put me in a foul mood.

When I got home from work last night, Dad was already stumbling around in a drunken stupor. I could see his silhouette through the window, and went in the back door so I wouldn't have to deal with him. What is the point of getting so wasted that you can't even walk? Even when I partied with my friends, before they turned into lovesick fools, I never allowed myself to get that out of control. It's one thing I'll never understand about my father. He needs help, and I hope one day he realizes that before it's too late.

On top of wondering if he was going to come into my

room to shout at me for something I didn't do, yet again, my alarm didn't go off. Either that, or I slept straight through it and it gave up on trying to wake me. I didn't even shower before I left for work. There wasn't time for all that. A quick rinse and brushing my teeth is all I managed before running out the door. And I forgot my lunch.

And now, I'm sitting in the parking lot of the deli and my car won't start. I should have left the car running after it gave me trouble this morning, but I didn't want to waste the gas. The stop was supposed to be quick. Grab something for me to eat for lunch and haul ass to work.

The clouds darken and a few tiny drops begin falling from the sky. Another spring storm is here to grace me with it's presence. My day is beginning to feel like that book we read in elementary school about that kid that had a horrible day. Bad things just kept piling up on him, and I've never felt more like him than I do now.

Lifting my foot up, I start to kick the tire again. It's not going to do any good. All that's going to happen is I'm going to bruise my foot. Instead, I open the door and reach below the panel to release the hood. It could be anything, the starter, alternator, or battery. Whatever it is, I'm hoping it's a cheap fix. The funds aren't there for yet another repair on this car. It's been good to me, getting me from point a to b. But, it's old, and starting to show its age with each passing day.

The rain is coming down a little harder as I lift the hood and look underneath, trying to find the source of my problem. One glance at my battery, tells me all I need to know. It's corroded with gunk all over the terminals. Batteries are expensive. At least it's a quick fix. All I need is a jump to get me to work and I can grab one as soon as I'm off.

"Is everything okay?" Her voice floats through the air. Jumping I hit my head on the hood, and curse. Amelia's voice shouldn't be recognizable to me. I'd be lying if I said I haven't thought about her since I saw her at work that day.

"Um, yeah. Just a little car trouble," I point toward the car with the hand that's not rubbing the bump that's already starting to form. That's going to hurt like a bitch later.

She's standing underneath an umbrella, prepared for the impending storm, smiling at me as if she doesn't have a care in the world. It's a far cry from last week. A huge weight has definitely been lifted from her shoulders, but she's still guarded. I can see in the way she eyes me. Cautious and curiously, as if she doesn't know whether she should be talking to me.

Finally, she speaks. "Is there anything I can do to help? I'm not great with car issues, Maybe I can give you a ride somewhere?"

Hopefully this isn't something she normally does, picking up strangers to cart them off to wherever they need to go. But, I don't need a ride. I only need this car to start to get me to work before I'm later than I already am.

"Actually, is there any chance you have a set of jumper cables?"

Cocking her head to the side, she runs a hand through her hair. She looks like a confused puppy, and it's more adorable than it should be. Stop it brain. Don't go there. She's off limits. Hell, everyone is off limits until I can get out of this town. "Maybe? I'm sure Uncle Jason has something in the car." She lifts the palm of her free hand. "Hold on a second, let me pull his car around, and we can see what he has in the trunk."

As if I could go anywhere unless it was my own two feet taking me. "Okay. I'll sit in the car so I don't get any wetter."

She hurries off toward the back of the lot. There's plenty of parking close to the store fronts, I'm not sure why she'd choose to park further from the door. Sliding into my car, I shut the door. It's not pouring yet, but it will be soon. Searching in the backseat of my car, I hope to find a towel, or dry shirt, anything to make myself somewhat presentable when I get to work.

It's not long before a car door closes next to me and Amelia is knocking on my window. The rain is coming down harder, and she's shivering. We aren't into the summer months yet, and even though we live in Texas, it's still on the cooler side.

She backs up as I reach for the door handle, giving me space to get out of the car. "I didn't see any cables in the front. I figured I'd look just in case." She presses a button on the key fob to make the trunk open. "I'm sure he has an emergency car kit in here somewhere, though. He's insanely serious about having things to help in situations like these."

I pull up the hatch that hides the spare tire except don't see a kit anywhere. Pulling my phone from my back pocket, I turn the flashlight on. There, in the very back of the trunk up against the backseats, a silver reflection is apparent when the light hits it. Thank you, Mr. Burgess for always being prepared. Amelia angles the umbrella to cover the both of us as I reach in to grab the bag. Cold drops of water hit my ankles as my jeans rise up since I'm halfway in the truck. For such a small car, I didn't think there'd be so much space.

Coming back out, bag in hand, I turn toward my car. Amelia grabs the bag out of my hand and points toward her car. "Let's get in and look at it. It's warm, and there's no sense in standing in the rain searching for the cables."

She walks around me toward the back door, leaving no room for argument. I could stay out here and continue to get wet while she looks for what I need. Or, I can get in the car. Realistically I know I should keep my distance, but I also don't want to offend her. She looks like she's in a good place right now, and I don't want to be the person to ruin it.

As soon as she sees me at the window, she opens the door and scoots back over. "Took you long enough. I don't bite, at least not anymore. Promise."

The door closes with a dull thud. The grin on my face is surprising. I remember what she's talking about.

Though it was so long ago, I don't know how she remembered. We were playing at Tonya's house and I took her doll away from her. Maybe I've always been a bit of jerk, even before my mom split. She bit me when I wouldn't give it back. We had to have been five or six years old. "I'm surprised you remember that."

"It's hard to forget when someone takes your favorite doll," she shrugs. "You picked on us girls a lot when we were younger."

I wince. Yep, I was definitely a little shit as a kid. Maybe Mom was right to bail on me, I couldn't have been easy to raise. "Sorry about that."

"No worries," she waves me off. "Cami punching you in the nose took care of any ill will I felt toward you." A small giggle escapes her lips and I want her to make that sound again. "It's all water under the bridge now."

"Thank you for helping me today. Most people would have kept walking." She makes me nervous. My hand lifts of its own volition to rub the back of my neck. I'm not sure what to do with my hands. It feels weird to just leave them lying in my lap. Crossing my arms would seem aggressive. This girl has me second guessing my every move. We aren't dating, or friends for that matter. There's no way I should be reacting to her this way. "What were you doing out here so early anyway? From what I remember you are a fan of sleep."

Every time we would go to Tonya's house, we were told not to come back until after lunch because they were still sleeping. It was annoying, but we always waited. We wanted to be there rather than our own homes.

"It's no problem, really." Amelia answers. "And, I was here applying for a job. I'm not sure how long I'll stick around. Ijust don't want to mooch off my aunt and uncle. I need to make my own way."

"Where did you apply?"

Instead of answering right away, she nods toward the deli. "There and that boutique store a few doors down." Pulling something out of the bag, she shouts in victory. "Aha, found it. I swear this bag is like that one Hermione has in the Deathly Hallows movie." She struggles to zip the bag closed after everything has been moved around. "How did they fit all of this in here and expect it to close again?"

"Let me see it." Pulling the bag from her hands, I push down and squeeze the sides tight. The zipper glides around with only a few hiccups on its journey. "I'll be right back with the cables. I'm going to pop the hood on here and jump mine off."

The rain is coming down even harder now. It wasn't noticeable when we were reminiscing about our childhood. But now, it pelts me with tiny stings. Rushing to the driver side door, I open it, pop the latch and close it again. As soon as I have the hood up, I hear a door open. She isn't staying in the car. Of course not. She's as stubborn as she was when we were kids. It must run in Mrs. Burgess's genes because Tonya is the same way.

I'm no longer getting soaking wet. I look up and the

umbrella is positioned to cover the both of us as much as possible. Putting the cables on her battery, I check to make sure they are secure. Running to my car, with Amelia behind me, doing her best to protect us from the storm, I attach the cables to my car.

Amelia's teeth are chattering and she's shivering. If she had stayed in the car, she wouldn't be cold, but I'm grateful she's thoughtful enough to want to keep me as dry as possible. "Can you go give your car some gas? I'm going to get in mine and try to get it to turn over."

"Doesn't it have to charge up, or something, before you do that?"

"Yeah. There's no sense in both of us getting wet to wait for that." A piece of hair is plastered on her cheek. A black streak across her pale face. My hand reaches up to her face. She doesn't shrink back. Her eyes are wide and full of wonder. Pushing the strand behind her ear, I let my fingers linger longer than necessary before pulling away. "If you give it gas, it'll charge faster."

I don't know if that's true, and I'll say anything to get her out of the cold. And to get my emotions in check. She doesn't argue. Running to get into her car she almost slips but catches herself. The umbrella closes and she gets into the driver seat, closing the door gently behind her.

Before opening my own car door, I shake my head. There's no way I can get involved with her. She said it herself, she's not staying around here. Neither am I if I can help it. Pulling the door open, I get in the car.

Once I'm safely inside, I glance through the window to see Amelia. She's rubbing her hands together in front of the vent, trying to warm them up. I hear her car engine rev as she presses on the gas. My hand is on the key to turn it, but she looks up and our eyes meet. Everything else falls away. The storm, all the shit I deal with on a day to day basis, being late to work, all of it fades into nothing. I have to get to know her. Not the girl she was when we were kids. The one sitting in the car beside me. The girl who has no doubt been broken is finding a way to put herself back together. I can't fight my attraction or my wonder. I'd be happy with friendship if that's what she's willing to offer me. As much as I've been trying, I can't deny that I'm interested in her.

Staring at her is starting to become weird. I can tell by her raised brows that she's waiting for me to do something. Then I remember, I'm supposed to be trying to start my car. I turn the key once, and nothing happens. It's the same result on the second try. Come on, please start. The third time's the charm. My car roars to life. I say a silent thank you to whoever may be listening.

Rushing to get the cables disconnected, I hop into the front passenger seat of Amelia's car. I let the jumper cables slide to the floorboard before turning toward her. She's beaming. "You did it," she exclaims.

"Thanks to you," I nod at her. "Seriously, thank you for helping me. I'd be missing a full day of work if you hadn't shown up."

"It's not a big deal," she laughs. "It's not like I had

anything else to do. At least I can say I saved a person today."

"Let me buy you dinner one night." The words tumble out of my mouth before I can think it through. What if she rejects me? Pursuing her seemed like a good idea moments ago, but now, face to face, I'm thinking maybe it's not.

"You don't have to do that."

"It's the least I can do. Please, let me thank you properly." When did I start using words like 'properly?' If Jake or Marshall heard me right now, they'd be laughing their asses off.

Amelia bites her bottom lip, worrying it between her teeth, and glances out the front window. The silence feels me with dread as the rain beats down on the car. She's playing with a ring on her pinky finger, turning it round and round in circles. Damn it, I just made her nervous. It takes all of my willpower not to reach out and ease her nerves.

"I'm not really looking for a boyfriend right now, Randall." Wincing, her eyes meet mine. "I appreciate the offer. It's just that I'm trying to get back on my feet, and dating would complicate that."

I throw my hands up in surrender. "We could go as friends. I'm not in any position to be dating anyone either." Not completely a lie. I shouldn't be considering dating anyone. It's the friend part that I'm bummed about.

What I just said must be working, though. She stops

playing with her ring, and squints at me. Trying to judge if my intentions are true. Shit, she's not going to trust me. There's no way she can't see my interest in her. Mentally crossing my fingers, I wait until she's done with whatever test she's hoping I'll pass.

"Okay," she relents. "I'll go to dinner with you. But only as friends. I could definitely use one of those right now. As much as I love my cousin and Reaf, hanging out with them makes me want to gag most of the time."

"I know the feeling," I chuckle. "Jake has Charleigh and Marshall has Bianca. It's worse when all four of them are together. And they wonder why I don't want to hang out with them more often."

"Right? There's only so many times a person can deal with people making doe eyes at each other."

"Agreed." I let out a breath. She said yes. On the outside I'm cool as a cucumber, on the inside there's a party going on. My heart is racing and my stomach is twisting in knots. In a good way, and now I'm more nervous than I was before she agreed to go out with me. Just friends, I repeat to myself. We're going as friends. Nothing more.

"Shouldn't you get to work?" She asks in the sudden silence. "If you don't go now, you'll miss an entire day."

"You're right," I say louder than I meant to. Reaching for the door, I pause. "Let me see your phone."

"What? Why?" Her nose scrunches up.

"So, I can text myself from your phone. Then we'll have each other's numbers. How else are we supposed to set up our evening of no longer being a third wheel if I can't contact you?"

"You have a point." She taps her chin. "You could always just stop by the house. I'm living with Tonya's parents right now."

"Uh, Mr. Burgess isn't exactly my biggest fan." I shrug. "It's nothing personal, he just didn't care for me after the whole thing with Jake. Though things could have changed now. He didn't seem upset that I was at the wedding."

"Yeah it was weird with Jake and Charleigh being there, but if it works who am I to judge." She smiles and hands her phone to me.

I take it, tapping out my phone number and send off the text.

When she sees it after I give her the phone, she snorts. "Friend in training, really?"

"Hey, maybe we both need practice in friendship." I glance at the time on the dashboard. "Shit, I need to go. I'll text you when I'm off work to set something up."

"Sounds good. Be safe on your way to work." Amelia motions to the rain still beating a steady rhythm outside. "You wouldn't want your new friend to be left with the lovesick puppies alone."

Nodding, I hop out of her car and into my own. Watching her pull out of the space beside mine and make her way toward the road, I dial the number to the store. Luckily, it's Tony that picks up the phone. "Hey Tony, it's

Randall. I'm on my way in now. The battery on my car died."

"Okay. Be careful, I heard some of the roads are starting to flood with all the rain."

"Will do," I reply.

"Seriously Randall, take your time. We've been pretty slow so there's no rush."

"Got it." Clicking end on the call, I can't stop the smile that takes over my face.

It looks like my day is turning around. My boss isn't mad, my car is running, and Amelia is going to have dinner with me. Who cares if it's only as friends? I can handle that. Right now, I feel like I can take on the world. Not even the rain can bring me down.

amelia

"I NEED to get my car here as soon as possible," I announce to nobody in particular as soon as I walk through the front door. My hair is a hot mess and beginning to curl from the rain. I didn't bother bringing the umbrella in when I got home, choosing to make a mad dash inside despite the downpour.

The house is quiet. I could have sworn Lucia's car was in the driveway when I ran in. Slipping off my shoes, I look around the corner of the entryway. Nobody is napping on the couch. Weird. Someone should definitely be here.

The walk to the living room is kind of creepy. The lights are off, and the lights on the cable box aren't even glowing. Shit, I guess the power must have gone out. Leaning over the couch, I take a quick peek out the window. My aunt's car is here. The outline barely visible with the windblown rain swirling through the air. Where the hell could they be? The couldn't have taken Uncle Jason's car because I've had it all morning.

The flashlight on my phone is the only way I make into the kitchen without tripping over anything. Lucia has a drawer in here somewhere that has a bunch of candles and flashlights in it. I'm not sure if that was her doing, or Jason's. More likely him since he seems to be prepared for every situation. I just have to find the right one. The contents of the drawer's jangle and move around as I open and shut them.

It's here, I know it. The house is almost completely black despite it being the middle of the day. The storm should have moved on by now. Or, maybe that's just wishful thinking. Storms have always creeped me out. Probably because we live in an area where tornadoes can pop up without a moment's notice. Either way, they suck. Pulling open the last drawer on the bar, I scream in victory. "Yes." Nestled inside are five big candles and two flashlights. I scoop up all the candles, the lighter, and grab one of the flashlights.

Setting two of the candles on the counter, I light them before flicking on the flashlight to find my way back to the living room. It wouldn't be so bad, but my aunt and uncle have decorative tables and art in really random places.

The last three candles are lined up in the center of the coffee table. Before lighting them, I scan the living room, trying to figure out what I'm supposed to do. The television isn't working, obviously, and I don't really have any hobbies. Flashlight in hand, I walk to my room. One of Tonya's shelves of books is still in here. I grab the first book my hand lands on. I have no clue what it's about, though it'll give me something to do until the power comes back on. Book in hand, I grab the blanket off my bed and head back into the living room.

Sitting on the edge of the couch, I lean forward and light the candles before setting into the corner of the couch. The flashlight is perched on my shoulder and couch so I don't have to hold it. The book cover is white with stripes and the title is written in orange. It's written by someone named Colleen Hoover. I've never heard of her, but I've also never been a big reader. Let's see what this book is about.

"Why are the lights off?" Aunt Lucia asks coming into the living room.

Crap. I fell asleep with the candles still burning. At least the house is still standing. "The power was out when I got home earlier." A yawn escapes me even though I just took an impromptu nap. "Where were y'all?"

Stretching, I stand up from the couch and the book I was reading drops to the floor. Hopefully none of the pages are bent. Tonya will kill me if they are. If there's one thing she values as much as her family, it's her books.

Uncle Jason is pulling his arms out of the sleeves of his jacket trying not to let any water drip on the floor. "Well, we were going to surprise you. Lucia even picked up cupcakes to celebrate."

"Celebrate what?" It's not my birthday, and I don't think there's any sort of special holiday today. Knowing them it's probably for a promotion Jason received. They celebrate every little thing, it's comical.

"Your new to you car," Lucia announces like she's a game show host.

"Wait, what? I already have a car." Maybe I'm still asleep and I didn't hear her correctly.

"About that," Jason steps in. "I talked to your dad yesterday, and they were going to bring it down next weekend."

"But..." I prompt.

He clears his throat. "But it wouldn't pass inspection and he said it wasn't safe to drive it this far."

"I love my car, though." And I do. It was old, and not in the best condition. It was mine, though. I bought it and paid for it with my own money. It was my baby.

"We know you do, sweetie," Lucia wraps an arm around me. "Right now, they have it parked until you decide what you want to do with it. In the meantime, we're giving you Jason's old car. That's where we were today, finalizing the paperwork on a new car for him."

"He didn't have to get a new car so that I could have his old one. That's not fair to the two of you." Inside I'm freaking out. Why would they do something so kind and generous? It's weird. Seriously, who does that?

"We know we didn't have to." Lucia rolls her eyes. "We wanted to. You're going to have places you want to go when we aren't available. And if you get a job, now you have a way to get there." Shrugging she continues, "Besides, Jason has been talking about a new car for months now. Why not kill two birds with one stone?"

"I guess," I drawl out. "But as soon as I get a job, I'm going to pay the insurance on it. You aren't going to foot the bill for that. And I'll also give you money to pay for the car." My aunt begins shaking her head at the last addition. "I will slip it into your purse if I have to."

"Fine," she mumbles. "Be difficult about it."

Motioning for Uncle Jason to join us, I pull the both of them into a group hug. "Thank you so much. It means a lot to me that you're consistently looking out for my well-being. You have no idea how much I appreciate it."

"We know, Melly." Jason pats my head the way he used to when I was a kid. "Now, let's go eat those cupcakes. I've been eyeing them the entire way home." This man is always thinking with his stomach.

The power is finally back on. It only took over four hours for it to happen. Lucia and Jason tried to keep me busy, except playing board games by candlelight gets old. Especially when they are super competitive and the games became about them. That might offend some people, but not me. It gave me the perfect excuse to slink off to my room and charge my phone.

So much has happened today. Between the new car, well new to me, and agreeing to dinner with Randall, my mind is reeling. I still can't believe my aunt and uncle were prepared to just give me a car. If that doesn't show how kind they can be, I don't know what will.

The display on my phone comes to life, finally having enough battery to do something on it. No messages. I didn't expect any, but I haven't talked to Tonya all day and she usually sends me some sort of meme to tell me how her day is going.

Opening up the text messages, I fire off a text that's sure to have her freaking out. Whether it will be good or bad will remain to be seen.

Amelia: I'm going out to dinner with Randall.
   Tonya: What!

Not even a second after my cousin's text comes through, my phone rings. "You cannot send a text like that without some kind of background information," she shrieks.

"Has anyone ever told you that you are overly nosy?" I laugh.

"No. Because I only butt in when I feel it's necessary."

Tonya's old bed is incredibly comfortable. Lying in it makes this conversation with her much more enjoyable because I know she's going to have a lot to say. "Which is all the time," I mutter into the pillow.

"What was that?"

"Nothing." Grinning I fluff my pillow until it's the perfect shape. "Besides, I was going to tell you, in the text message. That is before you called taking away the opportunity."

"Did you honestly think I would do anything different?" Tonya scoffs.

It would have been nice if she'd given me five minutes before demanding answers. I knew that wasn't going to happen. Now, I get to annoy her. "Did you know your parents gave me your dad's old car? He got a new one today. I'm paying on it regardless of how much they argue with me about it." The sentences almost run together. If I don't talk fast, she'll interrupt me.

"Yes," she groans. "I knew that. Who you think nudged them with the idea? Stop changing the subject." Tonya pauses. Waiting to see if I'm going to argue. I'm not going to because I'm grateful she thought about me enough to suggest it. "Now, spill."

"Fine." Sitting up, I lean against the backboard, and tell her everything that happened. From finding him kicking the shit out of his car to him brushing the piece of hair behind my ear.

I leave out the part about how I felt when he did it. Tingles raced up my spine and there was a spark for the few moments his fingers were on my face. Even though I know I can't date him, I wanted nothing more than to pull him closer just to see what his lips would feel like against my skin. His hair sliding between my fingers.

"Melly," Tonya screams through the phone.

"Huh?"

"Dude, what happened? You were talking and then nothing."

My cheeks flame even though I know she can't see me. "Sorry, just freaking out about dinner with him." It's partially the truth. It's not like I'm going to admit I was thinking about his hands on me.

"So, is it a date?" She thinks she's sly asking it all sweet and sing song like. She's not fooling anyone.

"No." Part of me wishes I didn't put the friend caveat on it, but my heart is thanking me for protecting it. "Just friends."

"Wow, I can't believe he was okay with that."

"Why do you say that?" Maybe I made a mistake in agreeing to dinner.

"He had a reputation in school." Hearing my intake of breath, she rushes on. "Though most of it was just talk. When girls would say he was out with them, I knew most of them weren't true because he would be at Marshall's house with the rest of us."

"So," I say, hesitantly. "You think this is a bad idea?"

"Not at all, prima." Layla's tiny giggles in the background make me smile. "I honestly think this will be good for both of you."

"That's good to know." My head falls back, and I wince at the pain. If Tonya condones it then it must be alright. There's no way she would let me do something that would hurt me in the end.

"I need to go." She shushes her daughter. "Layla is being stubborn, like Jake," she adds annoyed. "And refusing to lie down for the night. I'm going to see if reading to her will speed the process up."

Doing my best to cover my laughs, I say, "No worries. Give her lots of kisses from me."

"Will do. Talk to you tomorrow." Before I even get a chance to say goodbye, the other end is silent. Envy isn't something I feel for her. It has to be difficult holding down a job and going to school on top of everything else. Layla will be happy she has a mom who does so much for her.

Feeling better after talking to Tonya about the whole Randall situation, I set my phone on the nightstand and lie back down. Even if I don't get a call back from the jobs I applied for today, I can still look for one somewhere else. Especially since I have a car thanks to my amazing family.

My eyes are finally drifting off to sleep when my phone pings.

Randall: Hi, friend in training. ;)

. . .

This is a side of him I didn't think he possessed. He was so surly at the hardware store. Today wasn't horrible when I helped him, but he wasn't exactly this playful either. I don't respond to his text. Instead, I close my eyes and dream about a world of possibilities opening up before me.

randall

THREE DAYS. That's how long it's been since I sent Amelia a text message and she didn't respond. Not a single word. It was a little late, but most people our age aren't exactly the type to go to bed early.

Phone in hand, I waffle back and forth with whether I should text her again. I don't want to seem desperate, I can't help feeling that way. Any sort of human connection would be amazing right now.

Dad's been on a rampage. The guys have to be tired of hearing me bitch about all of my woes. Not that I do it often. It's been one of those weeks. I'm not sure my dad has even gone to work. He's home when I leave for work and when I get back. Beer in hand and television blasting.

Before my thoughts can take me too far off the deep end, I tap Amelia's name in my contacts. If she doesn't answer this text, I'll try calling her. After that, the ball to this friendship is in her court.

Randall: I'm not sure if my last text confused you, but it's Randall. Do you want to grab that dinner tonight?
    Randall: If you're free, that is.

Because that doesn't sound completely pathetic. There needs to be a way to recall messages before they travel through whatever path they take to the other person's phone. Someone needs to invent that as soon as possible. It'd save drunk texters everywhere.

Cringing at the last text, I set the phone in my work locker. It's a beautiful Spring day, and I have a feeling we're going to be insanely busy. Hopefully there will be a text waiting for me when I take my break. Until then, I have a job to do.

Work definitely hasn't let me down today. There's been a constant stream of customers, most of them wanting to get new plants for their flowerbeds. If I never see a potted plant again, I'd be completely okay with it. My pants have dirt and water stains trailing down them. Silently, I curse my fellow employees for choosing our busiest time of day to water everything. If these stains don't come out, I'll have to buy a couple pairs of new pants.

The break room is blessedly quiet when I walk in. The few people I share lunchtime with must have gone out to grab a bite to eat. That's a good thing, though. It's likely they'd witness me one of two ways, completely deflated or jumping for joy. I'd rather not have anyone see that. Not only would it be embarrassing, I also know they'd tell everyone within minutes.

The pull toward my locker is strong, and I'm terrified to open it. If my lunch wasn't in there, I'd delay opening it as long as possible. The fear of rejection is something I will most likely always deal with. My mom's rejection hit me hard and stays with me to this day. Then it was Tonya. I had a schoolboy crush on her, and I don't think she ever knew. If she did, she hid it well. The day she decided to date Jake, I was crushed. It hasn't escaped my notice that I'm interested in her cousin. It has nothing to do with Tonya, though Amelia's soul speaks to mine, and I feel the need to get to know her better.

Opening the small door, I reach past my phone to grab my lunch box. My fingers twitch to pick it up, but I pull the lunch bag out and close the door instead. The phone can wait until after I eat.

The break room table is old, and the corners are ragged from years of use. A jagged piece scratches my arm as I lean forward, taking my plain ham sandwich out of the insulated bag. One day I'll be able to afford more than simple sandwiches. Maybe even something that will fill me up instead of leaving me wanting more. Any extra money I have, I'm putting toward taking Amelia out to dinner.

There's a phone vibrating in one of the lockers, scaring me until I'm choking down the bite I just took. Could it be mine? Possibly. A part of me wants to jump up to see while the other wants to ignore it completely.

When it vibrates again, I set my sandwich down on a napkin. The chair screeches as I scoot away from the table. The phone is lit up as soon as I open the door and my heart tries to leap out of my chest. This is the do or die moment. The one that will have me screaming in victory or shoving my phone back into the locker.

Taking a deep breath, I swipe until the lock screen disappears.

Amelia: Sorry, I was already in bed and forgot to text back when I saw it.

Amelia: I'm free tonight, though. Just tell me where and what time to meet you.

A cry of victory echoes around the break room. It's a good thing nobody else is here. That would be embarrassing. If I wasn't terrified of someone walking in unexpectedly, I'd be dancing.

My fingers itch to text her back. I need to figure out where I'm going to take her, first. Fast food isn't an option, but I also can't afford something fancy. That doesn't leave many options.

Randall: Awesome. What are you in the mood for?

There. I've left the decision up to her. Even though cost is a factor, it'll be nice to spend time with someone who piques my interest. And who isn't in a relationship. Being the third wheel sucks.

Amelia: I don't know. I haven't been to very many restaurants around here. Is there a place that has good barbecue?

That's totally doable, and I know just the spot to take her. It's a local place and the food is absolutely delicious.

Randall: Barbecue it is. Are you sure you don't want me to pick you up? It's not a problem.

Amelia: Yes! It's been forever since I've had any. And I'm sure. That would be too date-like... and we're just friends. Remember?

. . .

Randall: Yeah, yeah. Just friends.

Amelia: Send me the name and I'll see you there around seven?

Randall: Sounds good. I'll text you when I get off work. My break is almost over.

Amelia: Have a great rest of the day, future bestie.

Closing out of my messages, I can't stop the huge smile that takes over my face. Tony walks in as I turn to put my phone back in my locker. "Your day must have gotten better."

"Yeah, it did."

"You sound happy," he grins. "Those days seem to be few and far between. To what do we owe this good mood?"

"I, uh, have a date." My cheeks warm.

"She must be special if you're actually going out without your friends."

"Very special." I place my phone in my locker and ease the door shut. "We're actually just friends. I hope to change that."

"Be careful." Tony's voice takes on a fatherly tone.

"Before you try to take anything further, you need to make sure you're both on the same page or it could ruin whatever friendship you may have."

"I will." It's not what I want to do, but I know he's right. He's the one that's been there for me when my own father is too drunk to care. "I'm going to get to work."

"If you need anything let me know."

"Will do." I open the door and walk into the store. There's absolutely nothing that can bring me down today. The countdown to dinner begins now.

* * *

The parking lot to The Pit is jam packed. I expected it, though and it's a testament to how good their food is. My stomach growls at the thought. It's been way too long since I've eaten well.

There's a car backing out of a spot and I put my blinker on to grab it as soon as he's gone. Amelia's dark hair and lightly tanned skin catches my eye as I put my car in park. She walks into the restaurant without a glance around her to see if I'm here yet. She walks with confidence while I'm nervous over even having dinner with her. Any hopes of bailing on dinner are dashed. I will not stand this girl up. I may have done it to the few girls in the past, not with her. She needs to know that she's special and not just a conquest. Or only "friend" material. She's meant for so much more.

Deep breaths. It's all I focus on as I turn off my car and open the door. I can do this. We're only hanging out. Nothing else. My stomach flips. I want it to be more. Maybe not right away, but in the future. We have the possibility of fixing each other.

The middle of Spring is not the time for summer weather to be sneaking in. I feel the heat trying to take over the mild temperature. It's par for the course in Texas, and I wish we had longer Springs before it feels like Summer. Quickening my steps, I make my way across the parking lot. Anxious to see Amelia.

She's standing right inside the door in front of the hostess stand. "I see you didn't chicken out," she deadpans.

"What are you talking about? I just got here." Shoving my hands in my pockets, I rock back and forth on my feet. I never know what to do with my hands. It feels awkward just letting them hang by my side.

"I saw you as soon as you parked." Her smirk gives me goosebumps. It's a good thing because it's been so long since anyone has made me feel anything. "I was beginning to wonder if you'd bail or not." She turns toward me eyes lifting until they meet mine. Her dark lashes are fanned out, and vulnerability pours from the look she's giving me. As if my not showing would hurt her.

"Wow. I didn't even see you look my way."

She shrugs. "I thought maybe if I came inside, you'd come, too... Eventually."

Her bravery in an environment she's not familiar with is amazing. We move up toward the hostess stand, and ask for a table for two. She grabs a couple of menus and utensils. "Right this way."

There's no doubt in my mind that tonight will be the highlight of my week. I'm going to cherish every moment of it.

amelia

THE HOSTESS LEADS us toward a table in the back. *The Pit* must be amazing, almost every table is taken. Who knew a place could be so busy during the week? Randall is walking next to me, and he bumps into me avoiding a chair. A spark shoots up my arm. A tiny part of me wants him to take my hand. For this to be more than just a dinner as friends.

The pain he caused me creeps in, and warns me that a relationship with a guy that pursues me without really knowing me is a bad idea. Chemistry is a hard thing to ignore, but I will do my best. My heart is on the line and I'd rather have him as a friend than boyfriend anyway. Friends can have fun together without any expectations. It's something I desperately need right now.

"Here you go," the hostess smiles. "Your server will be with you shortly."

"Thank you," I nod.

Randall rushes to my side of the table to pull out my chair before I sit down. The tips of my ears warm at the gesture. That seems like something someone would do on a date and I have to remind myself that isn't what's happening here. No other guy has ever done that for me, though. Well, except for my dad. "Thank you," I squeak before he takes the seat opposite me.

Randall grabs the menu, hiding most of his face. All I can see are his eyes as they scan the menu. At the speed they are going up and down the page, I'm not sure he's actually paying attention to it.

"So," I pick up my own menu, glancing over the options. Most BBQ places offer the same things, and I already know what I'm going to get. "How are things at the store? Anyone else dropping screws all over the place?"

Chuckling, he sets the menu down. "Nope. All screws are safe from your cousin's vengeance."

"I'm on Tonya's side here. Those screws attacked her." At his smirk, I relent. "Okay, she probably should have seen them. Honestly... Who leaves a box of open screws on top of wood?"

"You'd be surprised," he rolls his eyes. "A lot of times people will open the box to make sure it's the correct size before buying them. Or, they'll carry them around and place them wherever when they decide they don't need them or it's the wrong size for whatever project they're working on."

"They could at least put it back." This is a pet peeve

of mine. People can't be bothered to put things where they got them from when they change their minds. It happened all the time at the boutique I worked at back home. Drove me nuts.

"I agree," his shoulders lift in defeat. "But I deal with it. Today I was in the gardening section most of the time, helping people load soil and potted plants into their cars."

"Aw, that's so sweet." All I picture is Randall lifting huge bags into the cars of little old ladies all over town. It's probably not accurate, only I can't help romanticizing the whole the thing. His muscles rippling under his shirt sweeps through my mind, and my cheeks flame.

"It's my job. It's not too hard, and it makes the day go by faster when I'm constantly moving around."

"Good point."

A woman walks up to the table and stops right at the edge. "Hi, I'm Vickie. Do you kids know what you want?"

"Hello, Vickie." Glancing at the menu on the table one more time, I wonder what Randall will think when I place my order. "I'm ready. I'd like ribs, potato salad, and corn on the cob."

"Is that a half rack or full," Vickie asks before turning her attention to Randall.

"Um, half."

"I was going to get the same thing," Randall says. "Do you want to get a full and split it?"

"Sure."

Vickie writes it down on her small notepad. "Do you want the same sides?"

"Yes, except trade the corn for beans, please." He grabs the menus and holds them out for our waitress.

"What would y'all like to drink?"

"Sweet tea would be great," Randall answers.

"I'll have a Dr. Pepper, thank you." He didn't even bat an eye when I ordered the ribs. Most guys wouldn't have said anything, though they'd give you that look. The one where they'll keep silent, but wouldn't you rather have a salad or something. Just because I'm a girl doesn't mean I can't enjoy big meals.

"How's the job hunt going?" Randall asks as Vickie leaves to turn in our order.

"Pretty great, actually." Our waitress sets our drinks in front of us. Wow, she's quick. Taking a quick sip from my drink, I continue. "That boutique I applied at called me back." It's hard to contain my excitement. When I didn't hear back right away, I thought they may have hired someone else.

"That's amazing, Amelia," Randall says.

"Thank you. I'm pretty excited to be working again." Another sip of my drink. "It will give me something to do during the day. And... I'll actually have money to do stuff instead of relying on my mom to send Aunt Lucia money."

Asking Lucia and Tonya for anything makes me feel like such a bum. I'm not their responsibility. Hell, I'm not even my parents' problem anymore. I'm grateful for the help they are giving me until I'm in a good place again. Or, at least, a better place.

"I'm happy for you." Randall plays with the edge of his napkin. "It can be hard to find a job in small towns. What will you be doing?"

Dang it. That's the one thing I forgot to ask. "Actually, I don't know," I shrug. "I'm sure it'll be the usual, though. Stocking shelves, checking people out, and counting inventory. At least, that's what I did at the last boutique I worked for."

"So," he laughs. "Basically, what I do, but less sweaty and smelly."

"Exactly."

Randall looks like he's about to say something, except Vickie comes at the exact moment. "Here you go." She sets a plate with the biggest rack of ribs I've ever seen in the middle of the table. "I'll be right back with your sides and a couple of plates for y'all."

"Thank you." Screw waiting for the plates. I'm hungry. Plucking a rib from the rack, I take a bite and moan in satisfaction. "This is so good."

"I'm happy you aren't like most girls." Randall says as he reaches for a rib.

"What's that supposed to mean?"

He clears his throat. "Nothing bad," he rushes. "It's just that most girls will get a salad or some kind of small meal because they are too worried about what guys think of them."

"I like food, and food likes me." As much as I wish it

didn't sometimes. "I've never been one to base what I eat on who I'm around."

"That's a good thing." He shifts the plate of ribs to the side just in time for Vickie to set down our side orders and the extra plates. "Thank you, Vickie."

"If you need anything else, just holler." She gives a quick smile before walking to another table.

"This food is delicious," I mumble around a bite of potato salad. It's a good thing I'm not trying to date this guy because my manners have gone out the window.

"It's one of my favorite places to eat when I have a little extra cash."

My heart breaks. This is the type of place my parents and I would eat at, at least once a week. Curiosity is getting the best of me. I need to know what happened that this is a luxury for him. Now isn't the time ask, though. I'll save that for when I know him better.

* * *

"Do you need to go home right now?" Randall is walking me to my car. Only the two street lights in the parking lot illuminate the area. You would think a place as popular as this seems to be, there would be more lighting to ensure customers make it to their cars safely.

The wind blows bringing a chill that burrows deep. Spring is not ready to make room for Summer. I'll miss the cool days, but I'm ready for days spent at the lake and hanging out with my cousin. "Nope. I don't need to go home just yet."

"When do you start your new job?"

Shrugging, I wrap my arms around myself to stave off the cold air. "I'm not sure. I have to go by tomorrow to fill out some more paperwork. I'm sure they'll let me know then." I glance at him out of the corner of my eye. "Why? What's up?"

He shoves his hands in his pockets and lifts his shoulders until they are almost touching his ears. He's unsure, and I can't help finding it absolutely adorable. A guy being nervous around me is something new. The Jackhole was never anything but sure of himself. Comparing the two isn't smart, especially when I intend to be friends with Randall. I know this. Someone needs to inform the warm fuzzies that have taken up residence inside me every time he shoots a small smile.

"There's a park up the road. Any chance you would want to go?"

"In the dark?" I ask, shocked. Just because I've sort of known this guy since we were kids doesn't mean that I want to go traipsing around in dark areas with him. It's been years since I've been around him for any significant amount of time. He could be a sociopath for all I know. At the same time... Tonya would've said something if she though Randall posed any kind of a threat.

He laughs. "Yeah. It's actually more well-lit than this parking lot."

"Okay," I drawl. "Is there any chance you have a

jacket, or something, I can wear?" Waving my hands around, I emphasize my lack of anything warm. "I didn't exactly come prepared for an evening stroll in the park."

"Um, yeah. Hold on." Randall jogs to his car, quickly unlocking and opening the door before grabbing something out of his backseat. He lifts it to his nose, and turns toward me. Apparently, it passed the smell test. That's always a good sign.

My strides become longer as I try to make up the distance between us. There's no use in him walking all the way back here if we're going in the opposite direction. He shoves the wad of material toward me. "Here you go."

"Thanks," I say, shaking out it out until it loses its crumpled form. It's a hoodie instead of a jacket. The inside is plush, and I want to bury my face in it as I pull it over my head. I inhale deeply while adjusting the hood. It doesn't stink at all. Woodsy scents hit me in all the best ways. This smell is what I imagine that big guy in those paper towel commercials smelling like. I wonder what Randall would look like with a flannel shirt and beard.

"Amelia?" Randall's eyebrows arch. "Are you okay?"

Damn. He caught me drifting off into my head. Shaking my head, I turn toward him. "Yeah. I'm good. Are you ready?" The words rush out of my mouth.

"Yep. It's just up the block and around the corner." His shoulder bumps into mine. "Are you warm enough?"

"Uh-huh." For once I'm happy it's dark and he can't

see how badly I'm blushing. You cannot fall for this guy, Amelia. You're going to get your shit together and go back home as soon as you can. What if I find a reason to stay here? Nope. That thought needs to stop right there. As much as I love being around my family, I miss home.

Neither of us speak as we walk side by side to the park. Both of us in our heads and happy to exist in this moment. Knowing that we can let go of our fake happiness we flaunt in front of our friends. I could tell by his posture at the store the other day that he doesn't let his guard down too often. Tonight, though... Tonight it is as if he doesn't have a care in the world. That freedom looks good on him, and I envy his ability to completely let go. Even around someone new.

The swings sway gently in the breeze, and the clinking of the chains that hold them up gives the night an odd soundtrack. Not creepy or anything, but like the ticking hands of a clock. I assume he's going to lead me to them, and I'm shocked when he doesn't. The old rusty merry go round is his destination.

The metal creaks as he sits down in one of the sections, and pats the one next to him. Eyeing the old playground equipment, I gingerly take a seat and pull my legs up to my chest. The merry go round is cold, even though it was warm today, and I wish I would have worn jeans instead of leggings. It would have provided at least a little more cushion to protect my ass from the chill seeping in.

Randall keeps his feet planted on the ground and

leans back until he's lying down. The massive circle starts moving and I almost bump into the bars that section it up like a pie. The squealing is irritating, but it doesn't faze him in the least. Keeping my knees bent, I follow his lead and lie down. The sky is clear and the stars are sparkling. I can't remember the last time I took a moment out of my life to just stare into the sky and let my mind wander.

"What do you want from life?" Randall's deep voice breaks into the silence.

Wow, he's over here pondering the mysteries of life, and I'm worried about my ass getting frostbite. "Um, I don't know," I reply. "Lately, I'm trying to live day by day." I turn toward him. "What do you want?"

A long sigh escapes his lips. He doesn't look in my direction. "To be able to support myself and not clean up after everyone else." Now, he faces me, and I can see years of pain etched into his expression. "To be wanted."

What must have happened to make that one of the things he wants most in life? Don't get me wrong, I don't want to be alone. I've just never felt unwanted. My family has always shown me how loved I am. They are doing it now by letting me get over the bullshit that chased me away from home. Even if I was against it at first, they made the best possible decision they could for my well-being. It's definitely proving to be a good one.

"I think you're doing a pretty damn good job of taking care of yourself. You have a job, a car, and a friend like me." Winking at him, I smile so he knows the last part is a joke.

"It would be a lot easier if I didn't have to constantly take care of my dad. It's like he's the kid and I'm the parent. I'm so tired of being the adult."

"Randall," I reach over and take his hand in mine. "I'm so sorry. No child should have to take on the role of parent. What happened?"

He twines his fingers with mine. The feeling of *rightness* scares me, but I don't pull away. "I don't really want to get into tonight. Sorry I brought it up."

"It's okay. I completely understand." I give his hand a gentle squeeze. "Whenever you are ready to lift that burden off your chest, I'll be here. That's what friends are for."

His face falls for a split second and a grin appears just as quickly. "Exactly. I'm not *just* your friend... I'm pretty sure I'm at bestie level."

Rolling my eyes, I laugh. "If you say so."

"I do, and you can't take it back." The playful glint is back in his eyes, and I hope nothing ever takes it away. If our friendship keeps it there then I'll do my best to make sure he never loses it. He lifts our bound hands toward the sky. "You see those stars right there? That's the big dipper."

That's one of the few constellations I actually know, but I play along. Anything to keep that smile on his face. "You realize it's kind of hard to see when we're spinning, right?"

He lifts his feet off the ground and ducks under the bar until he's in the same space as I am. Putting his feet back on the ground, he stops the merry go round from going any further. "Is that better?"

"Much," I whisper, scared to disrupt the closeness between us now. No matter how much I tell myself this boy is off limits, I know I'm going to fall for him. We're on the same wavelength whether he knows it or not. The question now is do I keep fighting it, or give in?

We spend the rest of the night talking about everything and nothing. It's almost midnight when I get into my car and try to dampen the elation from spending time with Randall. The one person I'm beginning to feel like I can be myself around. That I don't have to put on a mask around.

One last wave through my window, and I turn the car on. There's no doubt who will be playing a leading role in my dreams tonight.

randall

MEMORIES OF AMELIA'S hand in mine plague my thoughts for days after our dinner. We've talked here and there. It's mostly been memes sent back and forth. But... we haven't seen each other since then. Our schedules haven't lined up and I'm getting antsy. Being around her is so easy. With her, I can forget that my mom left me and my dad is a drunk. She makes my life better even over text messages. My friends haven't been able to pull as many smiles, or genuine laughs, from me as she has.

My lunch breaks have consisted of me sending her as many laugh out loud funny memes as I possibly can before having to head back to work. My fingers are on the texting icon when my phone rings, and nearly falls out of my hand.

"I was just about to text you," I say as I answer the call.

"No more cat memes. I can't even with all the cute and funny," she laughs.

Shrugging, even though she can't see me, I respond. "And now I know your weakness. What's up? You usually don't call on your lunch break."

"What time do you get off work?" Her voice is high and excited.

"Six, today. Why?"

"Meet me at my house. We're going out tonight."

"Did you get a raise or something already?" From the few times I have seen her, she seems more like a home-body. Someone who hides away from the world instead of exploring it.

"Nope. I have a tattoo appointment with Jake's girl-friend and I don't want to go alone." She is quiet for a moment. "I mean as long as you don't have any plans and *want* to go with me."

Charleigh's uncle scares the hell out of me, but I would do anything to spend some quality time with Amelia. "I'll come with you. I don't think I would have gotten my tattoo if Jake, Marshall and Dylan hadn't been there with me. And if we weren't all drunk off our asses when we went."

"Yes," she shrieks through the phone, and I pull it away from my ear. "Wait... You have a tattoo? How did I not know this?"

"You never asked."

"Hmmm," she mumbles. I can practically see her tapping her chin in thought. "I need to be better at asking more questions. Be prepared for all the questions on the drive to Dallas."

"If I have to," I groan.

"Randall, your break is over. Get your butt out on the floor or I'll make you stay late," Tony barks through the now open door.

"Shit, I didn't mean to get you in trouble," Amelia gasps through the phone.

"Don't worry about it. Tony is just grouchy. He must not have had is afternoon dose of coffee."

Tony glares at me, except I see the upturn of his mouth and know he's full of crap.

"Okay, I'll see you later." She doesn't say bye, or anything. The phone goes silent and I'm left staring at it. Shocked *she* called *me* to go somewhere.

"I take it you have another hot date with the mystery girl," Tony asks as I put my phone and lunch box back in my locker.

"Not exactly a date," I inform him. "She wants me to go with her to get a tattoo. I'm the only friend she has outside of relatives."

"I'm pretty sure she thinks of you as more than a friend."

"How would you know, Old Man?" I joke.

"Because I see how fast your fingers fly across that phone screen when you are on your lunch break. Girls who want to be just friends don't reply that quickly. Unless... they are bored as all hell." He holds the door open.

"Thanks for the vote of confidence," I mutter.

"I bet you'll be officially dating by the end of next week. Now get to work."

I don't argue. I'll get to see Amelia in just a few short hours and I hope the rest of the day goes by quickly.

My hands are sweating as I direct my car toward the Burgess house. The last time I was here was for Tonya and Reaf's wedding. They've never been huge fans of me. It could be because I used to pick on Tonya when we were kids. If I had to guess, it's because my father is the town drunk. If he's not at work, or home for that matter, he's at the bar. Most people assume that I'm the same way. That I was kicked out of college for misbehavior. In reality it was to keep a roof over Dad's head. I want better than that for myself. I *deserve* better than that.

The house comes into view and for a split second, I consider turning around. Chasing Amelia is a mistake. I'm not good enough for her. She should be around someone that can give her so much more than what I can offer. What I should do and will do are two different things. I'm obviously a glutton for heartache.

Pulling up to the curb I put the car in park. Deep breath in and out. I can do this. We're friends. It's no different than our meme wars on the phone. Except... When I see her in person, I want nothing more than wrap my arms around her and kiss her senseless. I might as well get dumbass tattooed across my forehead.

Amelia is already running out of the house by the time I have my car door closed. She throws her arms around me. "Are you ready to go?"

"Well aren't you excited." Laughing, I squeeze her to me. For just a moment I imagine she's mine to hold like this. I release my hold before it becomes creepy.

"A little, but I've wanted one for as long as I can remember, and I have the money to do it now. Besides, it can't hurt that bad can it?" She's bouncing on her toes with anticipation.

"It didn't hurt for me. It wasn't exactly comfortable, either. It's hard to explain the feeling."

The gentle breeze lifts her hair, making her appear ethereal. She is stunning and I don't think she realizes it. She isn't wearing any makeup or dressing to impress anyone. Above all else, I'm happy that I'm someone she can relaxed around. It only makes me fall for her more and more each passing day.

"Will I be able to stop if it's too much?" Her eyes widened in shock as she asks the question.

If she is already having second thoughts maybe this isn't such a good idea. "I mean, you could. But it will look weird, especially if it's in an area that is visible." I take a moment to study her reaction. "Are you sure this is something you want to do?"

Amelia stands taller and pulls her shoulders back. "Yes, I want to do it. Getting a tattoo isn't something I decided to do on a whim. I have put a lot of thought into this, and it's something I need to do for me. A daily reminder when I'm having a tough time."

The small spark of doubt that flashed across her face seconds ago is gone, and I'm proud of her for taking the steps she needs in order to become who she wants to be. "Let's do this. Whose car are we taking?"

"We can take mine." She grabs my hand and begins pulling me toward her car in the driveway. "Would you be okay driving? I don't know the Dallas area very well, and I don't want to get lost."

I lead her around to the passenger side of the car and open the door for her to slide in. As she reaches for her seatbelt, I close the door and jog around the front until I'm on the driver side and getting in behind the wheel. "You want to get something to eat before we go?"

"Nope." Amelia pops the "p". "If I eat before we go, I may get nervous and puke on everyone. Nobody wants to see that." She scrunches up her nose in disgust. "And, that would be completely mortifying. I'd never be able to walk into that place again."

Before backing out of the driveway, I reach toward the radio to find a station for some music. As soon as my hand touches the knob Amelia slaps it away. "What the hell?"

"No music on the drive there. Remember? It's time for twenty questions." A conspiratorial grin takes over her face.

My head snaps back. "I thought you were just kidding about that."

She moves her hand in a circular motion telling me to get the car moving. "No such luck. You are supposed to be my best friend now, and I didn't even know you had a tattoo. I think in order for us to be on a true bestie level we need to know more about one another."

Putting the car in reverse I grown. "Do we really have to?" The glare she shoots me is all the answer I need. "What do you want to know?"

She taps her silver painted fingernail against her chin. "Hmmm, so many things. The most pressing matter, what is your favorite color?"

A smirk forms on my lips. Out of all the things she could ask me about, the first thing that pops out of her mouth is my favorite color. I stay quiet for a moment, keeping her in suspense, as if my answer could change the world. "Blue."

"Just blue? No specific shade?"

"No. Just blue." I turn on the blinker before merging onto the highway, our tiny town disappearing in the rearview mirror. "What else do you have for me?"

"Let's see." She stares out the window at the cars passing by for a few seconds before continuing, "What's your favorite food?"

"Tacos, hands down." She nods in agreement.

I notice brake lights up ahead and ease off the gas to begin slowing down. "What was your first job?"

"I've only ever worked at the hardware store. So, I

guess I'm still at my first job, with a small break when I went away for college."

"Why aren't you at college now?" Traffic has come to a complete stop, and there is nothing I can do to change the direction of our conversation. It would be nice to talk to somebody about it. My biggest worry is that she'll see how dysfunctional my family life is and will be done with me. Friendship, and anything else I had hoped for will be gone.

"Are you sure you want to know?" Amelia nods when I glance over at her. I let out a deep breath. Here goes nothing. "My dad has a drinking problem, and he'll get so far behind on his bills that he can't even make rent most months. Our landlord sent me a copy of the eviction notice he put on the door while I was at school, and told me unless Dad could come up with the rent by a certain date then he was going to have to kick him out."

The cars in front of me begin picking up speed and I take a quick peek at Amelia's reaction before I press on the gas. She's not running away screaming, so that's a plus. Not like she has much of a choice since we are on the highway, but it's reassuring that she doesn't have a horror-stricken expression on her face. "After I got that, I knew I couldn't stay there and leave him without a place to go. He may be a complete asshole most days. He's still my dad. I withdrew from all of my classes and came home to work."

Her hand slips into my own. "Where was your mom during all of this?"

That's something I would like to know as well. If it wasn't for *her,* we wouldn't have the issues that we do. We'd still be a family, and I wouldn't be terrified to let people in. "I don't know. She left us when I was around six because she didn't want a family anymore."

"Oh, Randall. I am so sorry." She sniffles as if she's crying. And when I look at her, a tear is streaming down her cheek.

"Don't cry, Amelia." I lift our joined hands to wipe the wetness away. "It happened a long time ago. And, as much as I wish I could go back to college it's just not in the cards right now. I'll be free one day, but until that day comes, I'll hope my dad will actually grow up and be a parent."

"That's something," Amelia's breath hitches, "no child should ever have to deal with. It's not fair to you. Did you even have a childhood?"

"Not really. I'm used to it, though." I squeeze her hand one last time before taking the exit toward Life in Ink. "It won't always be like this, and I'm lucky to have friends, especially new ones, by my side."

She pulls her hand out of mine, and crosses her arms over her chest. "It still pisses me off for you."

Changing topics while looking for a place to park, I ask, "Will you tell me what you're getting?"

A small smile curves her lips. "No. You'll have to wait to see the finished product."

Luckily there's a space in the lot next door to the

tattoo shop, and I whip in before anyone else beats me to it. "Well, I guess we better go in and find out."

"Let's go," she shouts into the small space. She gets out of the car before I have a chance to get to the other side to open the door for her. "I'm so excited."

She may be, but I see the nerves in the slight shake of her fingers. I'm not going to attempt to change her mind, though. Instead, I'll hold her hand through whatever pain she feels.

amelia

"THIS PLACE IS AMAZING." There is art covering almost every wall and door. This is my first time in a tattoo shop, and I wasn't sure what to expect. All the ones I've seen on TV are dingy and kind of creepy. Life in Ink is really nice. The lobby area is open with rooms off to the sides for each of the artists. I could sit in here and people watch all day.

"Are you surprised?" Randall whispers in my ear.

"Yeah," I turn to look at the paintings by the front window. "I was expecting something dark and not quite so inviting."

He laughs, and I can't tell if he's laughing with me or at me. "This definitely isn't one of those shady shops. People come here from all over to get inked by Charleigh and the others. She kind of made a name for herself when she first started."

"I can see that." There are a lot of people here with various conversations going on at the same time. If this is any indication of the wait time, I'm going to be here a while. Hopefully Randall doesn't have to go into work early tomorrow. It's most likely going to be a late night, and I don't want to be the reason he is exhausted. Not when he also has to deal with his dad's crap. Anger boils in me at the thought of how his dad treats him, but I'm going to try to keep it from consuming me. Randall asked me to drop it, and I will... For now.

"Let's go see Sophie," he nods toward the girl behind the only desk in the area. "She'll be able to see if Charleigh is free or not."

A small twinge of jealousy hits me when he says her name so casually. As if they are very familiar with each other. I have no claims on him. We're just friends, and I'm the one who's been so adamant that things stay that way. Besides, of course they know each other, they share mutual friends. I plaster a fake smile on my face, "Sure thing."

He places his hand on the small of my back and leads me toward the reception area. Warmth spreads through me at the tiny touch. This definitely isn't how someone would act if they were interested in someone else. At least, I don't think it is. I don't have the best experience when it comes to guys. Maybe I should give Randall a shot, and try the whole relationship thing with him. That's what he's been working for, and I'd have to be a fool not to see it. He goes out of his way to make time for me and to make me laugh. What more could a girl ask for? It's something I'll have to really think about.

"Hey, Soph," Randall leans on the tall desktop. "Is Charleigh around? My friend Amelia wants to get a tattoo." I cringe when he says *friend*. People who want to be just friends don't react so negatively to words like that. The realization that I like him as more than a friend hits me hard.

"Yeah," she says. She's not looking at Randall as she says it, though. She's staring at the room in the back corner of the shop. A guy with tattoos covering his arm can be partially seen in the doorway. His head is bent over someone, and I assume that means he's another artist here. I've never met him. Guess I don't need to worry about her having any sort of feelings for Randall. "She cleared a few hours for you. She's in there waiting for her. Do I need to show Amelia the way?"

"No, I've got it." He turns toward the left side of the shop, but stops. "You should just ask him out. Seeing you stare after him like a lost puppy is painful."

"One day," she sighs. She picks up the earbud dangling around her neck and puts it in her ear. She looks just as lost as I feel most days.

"Charleigh's room is over here," Randall grabs my hand and pulls me along with him. "I swear that girl is never going to make a move."

"Maybe she's scared."

"Possibly," he shrugs.

He might be scared, too. That could be why he's been okay with the friendship label we have. I don't have time to analyze this because we step through the doorway to Charleigh's work area. The room is silent. Charleigh, and Jake, are staring at us with their mouths wide open. "Um, hi," I wave.

Charleigh is the first to school her features. A wide smile replacing the look she had only moments ago. "Hey," she says excitedly. The pitch a tad too high. "Are you ready to get your first tattoo?"

"Yep." Why are they acting so weird?

Jake's mouth is still gaping. Charleigh puts her hand under his chin and lifts it until his lips are pressed together. "Close your mouth. It's starting to be creepy."

He shakes his head back and forth a couple of times. "Sorry." Waving his hands between us, he asks, "When did this happen?"

Randall snorts, "What? Are you my dad or something?"

"Noooo. I just didn't expect to see you here with Amelia." He's scratching his head in confusion.

"We're *friends*. And, she asked me to come with her." He's still holding my hand, and I'm getting irritated at his constant use of the word friends. Is it really that necessary to put so much emphasis on it?

"Do you know what you want?" Charleigh butts into their conversation. "I blocked out a few hours in case we needed to come up with a design for you since it's going to be on your body permanently."

"I know the word I want, but not the design around it." My palm is beginning to sweat, and thankfully Randall doesn't seem to mind because he keeps it firmly grasped in his own.

Charleigh wraps her arms around Jake and places a quick kiss on his cheek. "Thank you for dinner. I'll be home later."

"I can hang around if you want me to." He doesn't want to leave because he's trying to figure out if Randall is telling him the truth about us. I can see it in the way he keeps glancing between the both of us.

She glances at me for my opinion, and I shake my head subtly. "That's okay. We'll be fine. Besides, you have to get up early to go get Layla."

"Oh. Um, okay. I'll see you when you get home." His shoulders sag in defeat. There will be no juicy gossip for him.

While they say their goodbyes, I study Charleigh's work area. She has cute quote frames and other touches hanging on the walls. There are also art pieces that resemble a lot of the work decorating the waiting area.

"Did you draw the ones out there, too?" I point toward the main room.

"Most of them," she grins. "I had to fill up my free time while I was trying to prove I was ready to start tattooing. My uncle would critique each one and then hang them on the wall."

"They're really good." It should be illegal for people to have that much talent. I can't think of a single thing I'm exceptional at, but I hope one day I'm great at *something*.

"Thanks." She grabs a sketch book from the long table that lines the wall. "Are there any themes, or specific images that you like?"

Randall releases my hand and grabs the extra chair from the corner. "I feel like this is the perfect 'bestie' learning opportunity."

Charleigh laughs. "He doesn't have to be in here for this part if you don't want him to be."

Randall scoffs, and I giggle. "No, it's fine. He took time out of his day to come with me. He can stay."

"Okay, so themes, or objects, that you are drawn toward." She taps her pencil against her leg.

This is something I've never given a lot of thought. The only thing I've ever collected are dreamcatchers. I wonder if she can tie that into my design. "Well the word I want inked on me is hope. Is there a way you can incorporate that with a dreamcatcher, or even feathers?"

No response. I peek over at her and she's busy drawing. I'm excited to see what she comes up with, and nervous about actually going through with it. For a split second I wonder what my parents will say. They don't have any tattoos. They've also never said anything about my appearance. Luckily, I think I have some pretty cool parents.

"Why hope?" Randall asks from beside me, making

me jump. When did he get up? I didn't even see, or hear, him move.

"If y'all want a little bit more privacy, you can go hang out in front. Or even Bianca's area. I think she's taking a break." Her hand doesn't stop moving. "Just don't mess with anything. She gets bitchy when people touch her things."

"Good ol', Bianca," Randall mutters under his breath. I've only met her a couple of times, and I've been scared to approach her. She's really nice, don't get me wrong, but she has resting bitch face down to an art.

"We'll be back in a minute," I tell Charleigh before grabbing Randall's hand and pulling him out of the room. "Which way?"

"It's the one right next door," he chuckles.

"Oh, okay." I turn left and enter the door next to Charleigh's. This room is completely different than hers. It's full of pin-up posters and sugar skulls. There are no pops of pastel colors like there are in Charleigh's work area. Now, I only want to get know Bianca more. She seems like a pretty cool person.

Randall turns on the light, and takes a seat on the padded table in the middle of the room. Patting the seat next to him, he asks, "So, why did you choose hope as the word you want permanently etched into your skin?"

Sitting next to him, I keep my eyes on the floor and swing my legs back and forth. Right now, I feel dumb for letting a guy get in my head enough to make me run away from my problems. "There was a guy that royally screwed me over, and it destroyed me. He made a joke out of me and let his friends ridicule me to the point of packing up my things and moving here. He made me believe he loved me and threw it in my face by cheating on me, lying to me, and basically calling me a dumbass for believing I meant anything to him."

A tear slips down my cheek, followed by another one. Ugh, why am I so emotional today? That's twice in as many hours that I've cried. "Any chance I can go kick this guy's ass?" Randall asks and wipes the tears from my face.

"You can, but honestly, he's not worth it." It's something I realized after my conversation with Reaf, and I've been trying my best to focus on the good things since then. My mood has changed so much since I've started shifting my focus.

"Doesn't mean he doesn't deserve it." He scoots closer to me until our legs are touching and I can feel his breath on my shoulder. A shiver runs down my spine. This guy is getting to me in a way the asshole never did.

"True," I whisper. "I chose hope because it's something to look forward to. Hope for renewed strength, being happy with myself, and knowing I'll be okay when I go back home."

"You're already a badass in my eyes. You picked yourself up and left a toxic situation. Doing what is best for you, and that isn't running away. That's working toward being the best version of you." He places his hand on my knee and begins rubbing circles with his thumb. It's relaxing and I sink into his side. Grateful he doesn't think I'm a moron. "If anything, I wish I could be more like you."

"Randall, you're doing the best you can *right now*. You can't force your dad to change. He has to *want* to do it. All you can do is show him that you still love him despite his faults." I lift my face toward his so I can look him in the eyes and show him that I mean every single word.

His mouth inches closer to mine and my breath hitches. "Hey, are y'all ready?" Charleigh says from the doorway. "Oh, shit. I'm sorry, I didn't realize I was interrupting something." She backs out of the room slowly. "I'll just, um, go wait in my area." She's almost running the small distance to her workroom.

"Oh my God," my hands fly up to my face until it's completely covered. My cheeks and ears are hot and I can only guess at how red they are. This is so embarrassing. I know we didn't do anything wrong, or bad, but I figure we have roughly ten minutes before my phone starts blowing up with text messages from Tonya.

Randall gets off the table and pulls my hands down. He's almost squatting so that he can meet my eyes. "It's okay, Amelia. Nothing to be ashamed of."

"I know that," I mutter. "Maybe we should go in there before Jake calls you. I'm sure she's already told him."

"She's not like that," he reassures me. "She won't say anything to anyone until one of us says it's okay."

Nodding, I slide off the table. "Okay. Let's go see what masterpiece she has created for me."

We don't say anything about the almost kiss. Instead he grabs my hand as we walk to the room next door and gives it a quick squeeze. Charleigh is sitting on her stool, drawing a few more things in her sketch pad. When she notices us walk in, she holds up the notebook. "What do you think?"

My mouth opens, but no words come out. The drawing is stunning. It's a dreamcatcher and the word "hope" is written in the middle with tiny lines connecting it to the circle. Feathers are suspended from it and the tips are different shades of blue. She took my one word and created something remarkable. A work of art that will serve as daily inspiration for me.

"Is the silence good, or bad?" She glances from me to Randall. "I can't tell because I've never gotten that reaction before."

"Good," I croak past the emotion. "Very good. Where should it go? It's a little big for my arms, though. I want it in a place I can see it every day."

She glances at her drawing, "I can shrink it down if you want. But it would also look fantastic on your shoulder and upper arm."

"I don't want it so small I can't read it. My shoulder is fine."

"Sounds good. Let me grab my transfer paper so we can get this on you." She pulls out what she needs, grabs her stool and some earbuds, and begins going over the drawing again.

"Are you nervous?" Randall asks.

"A little," I reply. "You'll stay with me the whole time, right? For moral support."

His smile widens, "I'll hold your hand through the entire thing if I need to."

"I'll hold you to that."

"All done," Charleigh says. "Let's get this on you and make sure the placement is right."

She places the sheet on my arm and rubs it until she she's sure the transfer has taken. I walk to the mirror by the door to see what it will look like. The size is perfect and I can't wait to see what it will look like once it's there forever.

"All good?" She asks.

Nodding, I turn toward her. "It's perfect."

"Good deal. Take a seat in the chair, and we'll get started."

Doing as she asks, I sit in the chair beside the table. My arm on the armrest and anticipation running through my veins. Randall pulls the extra chair to the other side of me and takes a seat.

"The buzzing sound will start first. Then I'll start with one of the lines. It may sting at first, but try not to flinch."

"Okay." I turn my free hand up, an invitation for him to grab it. He doesn't disappoint, sliding his into my own. The buzzing begins and I wait for the first touch, willing myself not to move a muscle.

My eyes are set on the boy next to me. The person who's slowly putting me back together without even realizing it. I'm so completely lost in his dark brown eyes, that I barely notice when the needle touches my skin. Tonight, I'm throwing my reservations out the window. It's time he knows that I want to be more than his friend.

randall

THIS GIRL AMAZES ME. Her strength and determination to make a better life for herself is remarkable. "Are you doing okay?"

Charleigh has just finished all the major outlining on Amelia's tattoo. She still has to draw in some of the smaller lines, and that is where it can sometimes become painful. "Yeah, I'm good." Amelia winces when Charleigh pushes the needle in a little deeper into her skin.

"Good," I pat her hand in sympathy. "It shouldn't take that much longer. There are just a few of those tiny lines and adding color to the feathers, and Charleigh will be finished."

"I'm not that worried about how much time we have left. It really doesn't hurt that bad." She wriggles in her seat for a moment before she's on the other end of Charleigh's 'mom stare.' Considering she's not even Layla's actual mom, she's got it down pretty well.

Amelia is definitely a lot stronger than I am when it comes to pain. When I got mine, I thought they were going to have to tie me to the chair. I'm not about to tell her that though. Especially, after she's gone through this session with only a few twitches from the pain.

"So, what's good to eat around here?" Amelia asks Charleigh. "I'm starting to get hungry." As if to prove it, her stomach growls.

"Did you not eat before you came?" Charleigh laughs, and wipes away some of the excess ink.

"Um, I was too nervous to eat. I didn't want to lose my cool and end up puking all over everyone." She pulls her hand out of mine and waves it around as she speaks.

"Girl, you wouldn't be the first, or last, person to blow chunks in the shop. Do you have any idea how many drunk people we get in here every single day?" She gives me a pointed look. After all, that's how she met Jake. We showed up here after a night of drinking to get inked together.

"That is a very good point," Amelia runs her hand through her hair, unable to be still. "Now, I feel like a moron for not eating before we came."

"I'll only need about twenty more minutes, and then you'll be able to eat." She's coloring in one of the feathers. "There's a really good hamburger place right across the street."

Jake and Marshall told me about that place. Jake described it as "food so good you'll want to slap your mama." I'm pretty sure he actually did want to slap his mom because at the time she was being downright ridiculous. "Why don't I run across the street and place a to go order so that it's ready when you are done?"

"Good idea. I want a hamburger, medium well, with mustard, and everything on it except onions." Amelia taps her finger on the side of her cheek, making sure she didn't forget anything. "Oh yeah, and fries with lots of ketchup."

"Okay, I'll be right back." Taking a couple of steps toward the door, I turned back around, "Charleigh, do you want anything?"

"Naw, I'm good," she continues working on Amelia's tattoo. "We'll be here when you get back."

Instead of waiting for either of them to say anything else, I walk back toward the door. If we thought there were a lot of people in the lobby earlier, that's nothing compared to now. There isn't an open seat in sight, and I have no idea how all of these people are going to be seen within the five or six hours before the shop closes. I guess, it's a good thing at least two of the artists' work quickly. The other shops better watch out, Life in Ink is on the rise.

There are even more people waiting outside when I open the door. It baffles me that the shop has become as popular as it is. Since all the artists have started working as a team, and stopped bickering with each other, the shop has been able to run a lot smoother. Sophie coming on as a receptionist has helped, too. Or, at least that what Jake tells me. Anytime him or Marshall are around

Charlie and Bianca, they get the lowdown on the drama at the shop. Which is how I know about Sophie's crush on Adrian. One of them needs to make a move. The tension is driving me crazy, and I'm not even around it all the time.

The night air is warm and sticky, and I'm thankful I was able to find a parking spot in the lot next door to Life in Ink. We won't be sweating so much when we leave. The place Charleigh was talking about is literally across the street. If I didn't have to wait for the crosswalk sign to change, I would already be over there. Finally, after a few long minutes, the walking sign begins to flash. There are a lot of people out tonight, and I'm being jostled in their rush to get to the next place.

The restaurant is busy when I walk in, but most of these people are waiting for a table. There is an area at the bar set up to take carryout orders. A guy not much younger than I am stands behind the register staring at his phone. "Excuse me, I'd like to place a to-go order."

He doesn't acknowledge me, and acts like I'm not even there. As someone who has had to work for far longer than I should, I have always taken pride in my work. If one of the customers in the store needs my help, I do my best to help them. Already, this place is on my list of restaurants to not visit again. The only saving grace, is the red-headed lady that comes out from the kitchen and smacks the guy in the back of the head. "Hey, you have a customer standing right in front of you. Either put your phone down and get to work, or go home and don't come back."

He doesn't say a word, he turns around, heads to where the kitchen is, and leaves. "Stupid teenage punks," the waitress says under her breath. "Anyway, what can I get you? Sorry about the lack of service." She glares in the direction the kid went. I don't feel bad for him in the slightest.

"It's all good. I need two burgers, medium well, with mustard, and everything except for onions. I also need 2 orders of fries."

"Anything, else?"

Tapping my fingers against the bar top, I try to remember if they wanted anything else. "No, I think that's it."

She reads the order back to me, and I almost freak out about the cost. But this is Amelia's night, and I'll do anything for that girl, including spend all my money. Luckily, the order won't take too long, and I'll be on my way in a bit.

Thinking back to the last time we went out, I try to remember if she ate onions while we were there. I'm almost certain she did. There's only one reason, besides not liking them, a person wouldn't get onions on their food... Kissing. My fingers are crossed and I can't wait to get back to her. Charleigh walking in on our near kiss has had me antsy to get Amelia alone again all night.

Maybe tonight is a turning point, and she'll stop trying so hard to push me away. She *has* to know by now that it's not going to work. Patience is something I'm very good at. You kind of have to be when you live in my house.

"I have a to-go order for Randall." One of the employees calls out. The place is so noisy that I almost don't hear them.

Shockingly, it didn't take long for them to have my order ready. Or, I glance at my cell phone to check the time, I was too busy thinking about kissing Amelia that I didn't even notice the time passing by.

Taking a few steps between the chairs where I was sitting and the bar, I let the waitress know that I am here. "I think this order belongs to me. I'm Randall."

This waitress is much younger than the one who took my order, and unless my eyes are deceiving me, she's checking me out. Normally, this wouldn't bother me but I've got a gorgeous brunette across the street waiting on me.

"What are you doing later tonight?" She asks, boldly.

"I'm sorry. I'm taken." So, what if that isn't technically true. It's very close to being a fact. I can feel it in my gut. The girl standing behind the counter doesn't need to know that though.

"That's too bad," she pouts. This girl and I don't even know each other, and she's acting as if me being involved with somebody, is a huge disservice to her. Nights like this remind me why I didn't date for so long. I can't handle all the petty games. I've always had better things to do, or work, that kept me busy anyway. At least, until her.

"Have a good night," I say, brushing the waitress off. Making a beeline the door, I don't look back. Any sort of encouragement with this girl is bound to lead to trouble, and that is something I don't need right now.

I hear my name being called from behind me, and I quicken my pace to the curb. Lucky for me, the crosswalk symbol is flashing and I can make a quick getaway before she does something crazy like follow me.

The crowd outside of Life in Ink has dispersed. Their hopes of getting inked tonight dashed when they saw how many people were inside. Or at least, that's what I'm assuming. Sophie is sitting at the desk, doodling on a notepad when I walk into the shop. She doesn't even look up when I come in. It's odd, but I'm not worried about it. Instead, I turn toward Charleigh's work room, and run smack dab into Amelia. The bag of food slips from my hand, and almost falls to the floor. I get a grip on it at the last possible second. There's no way I'm going to let this food go to waste.

"Shit," Amelia screeches. "I'm so sorry. I was coming to see if you were back yet, and wasn't paying attention. Are you okay?" Her hand circles around my wrist, the tips of her fingers nowhere near touching. It's as if she's trying to keep me steady with the loose grasp, and I can't help but like her even more for that.

"Yeah, I'm good." I lift the bag of food in my other hand. "I saved the food."

"That's obviously the most important part," Amelia rolls her eyes. "Are you ready to go?"

"Not until I see the finished product," I argue.

"It's all wrapped up. You'll have to wait a bit to see it. Maybe we can find somewhere to eat and I'll show you afterward." She touches the edge of the plastic around her tattoo. "Thank you, again, Charleigh. It's more than I could have dreamed up. I seriously can't wait until it's healed."

"Anytime, girl," Charleigh grins. "Let me know when you want to come in for the next one. I can tell by the look in your eyes that you're already itching for it."

"You know your clients well," Amelia laughs. "I'll be calling you soon. Now... I'm going to go eat. I'm starving."

"Y'all be careful on the drive home."

"We will," I say. "Tell Jake I'll call him tomorrow sometime."

Charleigh has a shit eating grin when she replies, "Will do. Don't do anything I wouldn't do."

Rolling my eyes, I turn toward the shop door, and place my hand on the small of Amelia's back. I want to pull her closer. Not until I know for sure that we're on the same page, though That I'll have the right to hold her in my arms and not let go.

I open the car door for her before I slide into the driver seat. "Want to go back to the park? It's not too cold tonight."

"Sure," she says as her stomach growls again. "Can

we eat the fries on the way there? Cold fries are never good, and I'm pretty sure my stomach may start eating itself if I don't feed it."

"Go ahead," I hand over the bag of food. "I'll get us to the park as fast as possible."

"I think this is going to become *our* spot," Amelia says around a mouthful of hamburger. That would probably gross most guys out. I think it's kind of cute.

We're sitting on the merry go round again, not spinning this time because that's just asking for trouble. There isn't much room for talk. Amelia is eating like she's been starving for days. Most of it has to be from adrenaline, though. She keeps lifting up the small sleeve on her shirt to admire her new ink. I get why people like them, and go get them frequently, it's just not my thing. One is enough for me.

This should be the perfect segue for the talk I want to have about us. I chicken out. "How's the burger?"

"So, freaking good," she moans. "It probably would have been better when it was still hot, but the temperature doesn't matter at all. It's. That. Good."

Charleigh is a goddess for mentioning that restaurant. If it were up to me, we would have hit up a drive thru on the way back to Asheville. "I'm glad you like it," I smile. As long as she's happy, I'm happy.

She crumbles the wax paper holding the burger and

shoves it in the bag. "I can't wait to take this stupid wrap off. It's starting to itch."

"Whatever you do, don't scratch it. It could take the ink off your skin."

"You know," she leans back. "For someone who doesn't have a lot of tattoos, you sure know a lot about them."

Wrapping the other half of my burger up, I place it in the bag. It'll be my lunch at work tomorrow. "It's the hazard of having two best friends that are dating tattoo artists." It's literally all they talk about some nights. I could probably run that shop if they ever needed me to.

"What time do you have to go to work tomorrow?"

"Early," I reply. "I have to open."

"And here I am keeping you out late." She looks over at me. "You can take me home if you need to since you have to be up super early. I don't go in until lunch."

The urge to tell her it's fine is strong. Being tired, and grumpy, is almost worth it if it means I get to spend more time with her. She makes me feel *lighter*, like I don't have a shit hole home to go back to. On the other hand, Tony doesn't like when I'm overly tired, and is likely to send me home if he sees me so much as yawn.

"Are you sure? I don't want the night to end. I have no idea what's in store for me tomorrow." It kills me to say that.

"Yep. I'm good. I could probably use more sleep. It's still hard for me to fall asleep in a room that isn't mine."

She grabs the food bag and starts to stand up. "Are you done with this?"

"I have the rest of my burger in there. I can take that out so we can put the rest in the trash." I reach for the bag.

"Or," she pulls it back. "I can take my trash out and you can keep the bag so it doesn't fall apart in the car."

She pulls the wrappings from her burger out of the bag, and I follow her to the trash can before walking to the car. We're halfway to the parking lot when Amelia starts running. "What are you doing?"

"Racing you, duh. What does it look like?"

What the hell? "Aren't you generally supposed to get a heads-up, or at least a countdown?"

She's less than a yard from the car when she slows her pace. "I assumed me running was a pretty good indication."

"I'm not a mind reader," I laugh. "I thought something was chasing you."

She reaches the car, and throws the door open. "What in the world could be chasing me? There's literally nothing out here except the two of us."

I finally reach the car, and get in as she closes her door. "I don't know. A rabid squirrel, a snake. It could be anything. Just because we are *in town* doesn't mean there isn't wildlife."

"Good point," she nods. "I'll have to remember that the next time I beat you."

"You didn't beat me," I huff. "If I had known it was a competition, I would have left you in my dust."

Putting the car in drive, I glance over at her. She's looking at me as if I've offended her. "Excuse me, I can beat you a hundred times over."

"I guess we'll have to have a rematch, then." It shouldn't be this much fun getting under her skin. She's cute when she's mad. Hell, she's cute no matter what.

The drive back to her aunt and uncles doesn't take long. The roads are vacant of other drivers, and Taylor Swift is singing about it being too soon on the radio. My fingers itch to change the station, but Amelia is silently mouthing the words and I don't want to turn off something she obviously likes.

All the lights are off in her house, and the quiet is comforting. She gets out of the car and I follow suit since mine is still parked along the curb. She doesn't go inside like I expect her to. Instead, she leans against her car looking up at me beneath her long lashes. "I'm sorry about freaking out earlier."

"What?" I'm not sure what she's talking about. It's not like she spazzed out while getting her tattoo.

"About the kiss," she whispers. "It was spur of the moment, and if you don't want that to happen, I completely understand."

The uneasiness in her voice pisses me off. That douchebag put doubt in her mind for any future boyfriends she may have. She's beautiful, caring, and so much fun to be around. If he didn't treasure her, that's his loss. I'm going to take my opportunity now, and do what I told Sophie to do. "I'm going to kiss you now. Is that okay?"

She nods, and I don't hesitate. Placing my hand on her cheek, I brush away the hair that's fallen in her face, and lean in. Her lips are soft and hesitant. Uncertain if I'm doing this because I want it or because she wants it. Deepening the kiss, I wipe away any reservations she may have. Her tongue sweeps across my lips and I grant her entrance.

I'm not sure how long we stand against her car, kissing each other as if it's the only way we'll take our next breath. She pulls away. "That was," she mumbles. "That was... wow."

"I literally have no words." And I don't. Kissing Amelia is everything I hoped it would be, and so much more. This is where I belong. Most people don't believe in love at first sight, but I knew the minute I saw her over Christmas break, I belong by her side.

"Goodnight, Randall," she gives me a quick peck and rushes into the house.

My feet don't move from their spot. She kissed me and dashed. I'm not sure that's ever happened before and I don't know what to make of it. Is it a good thing, or bad?

I get my answer as soon as I start my car. My phone pings with a text.

Amelia: I had fun tonight. Thank you for tagging along

with me to get my first tattoo. ~ Your BFF, and hopefully girlfriend. ;)

There's no hopefully about it. That's all the confirmation I need to know that she feels the same way about me.

amelia

DID THAT SERIOUSLY JUST HAPPEN? I press my fingers to my lips, and grin. The ghost of his kiss is still there, and it's the only thing I'll think of for the rest of the night. First... I need to call Tonya. The urge to tell someone is hard to ignore, and she's the only person I want to tell right now. Who cares if it's almost midnight? She'll understand, I hope.

Digging through my purse, I search for my phone. The damn thing was just in my hands a few minutes ago. Ugh, I hope the text I sent him didn't sound desperate. Worry forms in the pit of my stomach. Maybe it was too soon for the *girlfriend* statement. No. I will not let doubt and insecurities plague my thoughts. He likes me. I could feel it in the way he kissed me. He wasn't doing it to make me feel better about leaning into him earlier. I have to believe that. There's no way I could fall for two complete assholes in such a short amount of time. Is there?

Where is my phone? I could have sworn I put it in here. My fingers only graze candy wrappers, lip gloss, and hair ties. Setting my purse on the desk, I begin patting my pockets.

Aha. There it is. Nestled in my back pocket where it usually stays. I've gotten in the habit of putting it in my purse when I'm with Randall because I don't need it when I'm with him. The distraction of scrolling through news feeds doesn't appeal to me when we're together. We have a great time, and there's no reason for me to pull out my phone.

My excitement deflates when I don't see any new messages on my lock screen, but I brush it aside. He's driving and a response from him can wait until he gets home. Opening up my contacts, I search for Tonya's name on my favorites list and tap it to call her.

A loud ringing pours through the receiver. Come on, cuz, answer the phone. When the call goes to voicemail, I hang up before leaving a message. She's never not answered the phone when I call. Even when it's the wee hours of the morning. Bummed I throw the phone on my bed and change into my pajamas. Well, pajamas is a stretch since I sleep in t-shirts and shorts. They are comfortable, though and I don't need anything fancy to sleep in.

My shirt catches on the wrapping around my new tattoo serving as a reminder to take it off. I'm not even sure how I forgot about it, but then I remember the kiss and have my answer. Those few moments with Randall, his lips on mine, took over every brain cell I possess.

Slowly pulling the plastic off, I admire the work of art that is now a part of me forever. The colors on the feathers are vivid and the lines are so intricate. I'm amazed at the talent Charleigh has. Tonya told me that she was good, but I didn't realize what an understatement that was. She is phenomenal, and I'm sure the sudden increase in traffic at the shop has a lot to do with her.

My phone rings as I wad up the plastic and throw it in the trash. The quick dash to the bed to answer it before it wakes my aunt and uncle up results in me hitting my shin on the bed frame. Shit, that's likely to leave a bruise tomorrow. "Ow. Hello," I gasp into the phone as I bring it to my ear.

"You had better be stranded on the side of the road, or in some sort of crisis," Tonya whispers loudly into the phone. "Do you have any idea what time it is?"

"Sorry, grandma," I snort. "I didn't realize you were on a set schedule."

"Jokes about me being old will get you nowhere." A door closes on her end of the call, and I'm pretty sure she's walking to the living room so she doesn't wake Reaf or Layla. "Seriously, are you okay? Do I need to come pick you up from somewhere?"

"No," I laugh. "I'm fine."

"Then why are you calling me so late?"

"Why are you being so crabby?" I snap back. "You've never had any issues with me calling you this late before."

"Sorry," she mumbles. "Layla has been fighting us when it comes to bed time, and getting up ridiculously early. I'm exhausted."

"Damn," I say, sitting on the edge of my bed. "That has to be rough. I'm sorry for bugging you." And the worst cousin of the year award goes to me. It's still hard for me to remember that she has a family, and more responsibilities, now. She can't drop everything to answer my middle of the night calls like she could when we were still in high school.

"It's okay," she replies. "Who needs sleep anyway?"

"You do."

She sighs, "That's stating the obvious." A few seconds of silence pass. "So, what's up? You usually only call when you have something you need to get off your chest, or you can't sleep."

"I kissed Randall." The words tumble out of my mouth in a rush.

"You did what?" My cousin shrieks. She clears her throat and whispers, "You kissed Randall?"

"Well," I draw out. "He kissed me. It was totally mutual."

"Back up. How did this kiss come about?"

Do I give her the whole story, or just fill her in on the good parts? Might as well start at the beginning. "I asked him to go to the tattoo shop with me, and we had an almost kiss while we were there until Charleigh walked in. I was so freaking embarrassed. When we got back to the house, he asked if he could kiss me." Just thinking about how he asked before going in for the kiss makes me swoon all over again. For all the crap I've heard about him, he turned out to be such a gentlemen about the whole situation.

"And, I'm assuming you said yes?" It sounds more like an accusation than a question. She didn't have any problems with me being his friend. Why would she object to the possibility of it turning into morel?

"Well, yeah," I say. "Otherwise, I wouldn't be calling you to tell you about it."

The quiet coming from her side of the line is unsettling. I have this big balloon of happiness, and excitement, and I feel like she's about to pop it. My cousin is going to force me to drift back down to reality. A place I'm not sure I want to be. For once, after all the crap I've dealt with, I just want to be *happy*.

"Look," she finally speaks. "I have nothing against Randall. He's had a shitty life," I can already hear the "but" that's coming, even as I do my best to will it away. "but... do you think it might be a little soon for you?"

"Soon for me in what regard?" Playing dumb isn't something I normally do. "He's a guy that genuinely likes me and makes me laugh. I'm not sure I see a problem."

"You know what I mean, Amelia," Tonya's voice is matter of fact, brooking no argument. "Just a few weeks ago, you were curled up on my couch, hiding from the world. Hell, hiding from your own family. I only want to make sure you're doing what's best for you."

Her brutal honesty hits me in the gut. She's not trying to be mean, I know that. I've been hiding from the world way too long. Before I dated Andrew, I stayed to myself. Not wanting to take a chance on anything. Perfectly happy with the status quo. After he destroyed me, I hid away again. If I actually want to *live*, I need to open myself up to possibilities.

"For once in my life, I think I'm doing the right thing." Flipping over to my stomach, I lean on my elbows. "Andrew did a number on me, I won't lie about that. Letting the awful, and hurtful, things he did taint my future isn't good either."

"Then I support whatever makes you happy," Tonya relents. "No matter what happens in the future, just know that I'm here for you either way. I've always got your back."

"That means a lot," I breathe a sigh of relief. "Plus side, I'll no longer be the third wheel in group settings."

"Is that really how we make you feel?"

"Sometimes," I shrug even though she can't see me. "I was okay with it. If I wasn't actively included, it gave me a chance to shrink into myself without being a bother to anyone."

"I'm so sorry," my cousin says. "That's not how we wanted to make you feel. We can cut back on all the lovey-dovey stuff if it makes you feel better."

"Dude, no. You and Reaf need to continue being your

disgustingly cute selves. If anything, your relationship inspires me." I flop onto my back. My arms are starting to fall asleep, and have that weird tingly feeling in them. "I want what you have one day."

"And you think you'll find that with Randall," Tonya questions.

"Maybe. Maybe not," I sigh. "I'm willing to see where it goes."

Tonya yawns, causing me to yawn in return. "Do you want to keep talking?"

"Naw," another yawn escapes. "I'll let you get back to sleep. Bring Layla into the shop tomorrow. We just got a new batch of adorable dresses."

"I will," she agrees. "I've been looking for some clothes for the summer. This child is growing so quickly I can't keep up with her."

"She's going to be the most stylish little girl in town," I say. "Goodnight, Tonya. Thank you. For, well, everything. You truly are one of the best people in my life."

"Night, Melly. Call me anytime," she takes a breath. "Even if it's in the middle of the night to talk about a kiss. I'm always here for you."

She ends the call before I get a chance to do it first. A message came through while I was on the phone, and my heart starts pumping faster.

• • •

Randall: Thank you for inviting me. And, there's no hopefully about it. You're stuck with me for as long as you want me. Goodnight, Beautiful.

My fingers itch to text him back. The only thing that keeps me from doing it is knowing he has to wake up early in the morning for work. Or the fact that it's after one in the morning. How did time pass so quickly while I was on the phone? Normally I'm not one that enjoys phone conversations. It's a task that I've always hated. My preference is almost always text messages. There are no weird, or awkward, goodbyes. You just stop texting. Even with my aversion to actual conversations, it was nice talking to Tonya. It almost felt like when we were little girls and would stay up late talking about our crushes, or any other huge event happening in our lives. That hour-long phone call made me feel closer to my cousin than I have in ages.

Setting my phone on the nightstand beside my bed, I can't stop the wide smile taking over my face. For the first time in a long time, I feel like everything is going to be alright. My life is lining up to be something spectacular, and I'm worthy of someone else's affections.

A small part of me knows that I shouldn't place value on myself according to what others think about me. Randall likes me for exactly who I am without trying to change me into something else.

My alarm is set, and I'm ready to take on whatever

life has in store for me. Falling asleep should be difficult with my thoughts bouncing around like the little balls in a pinball machine, but soon my eyes are drifting shut, and the last thing I think of is the kiss I shared with Randall. And the promise it holds for what is to come.

randall

AMELIA and I have been inseparable since we became a couple. We hang out at her house, the park, Tonya's, or Jake's. My house is the one place I refuse to bring her. Dad has gotten worse. The words are sharper, and the punches are harder. It's been years since he's gotten physical with me, and I can't say that I miss it.

Even though I don't fight him when he's acting like an asshole, restraining him is taxing on my body. I have bruises along my ribs from trying to keep his arms pinned to his sides. He somehow always manages to elbow me when I least expect it. When I was younger, I would leave until I knew he was passed out on the couch. But now... I worry he's going to hurt himself when he's in his drunken stupors. If I could figure out what has set him off these past few days, I'd do anything I can to prevent it. I know the time is coming to have a talk with him. He has to stop letting mom's actions in the past dictate how he lives his life *now*. He used to be happy, and I want that for him again. I'll talk to him this weekend when I actually have a day off. Maybe he'll be sober enough to have adult conversation. He needs help even if he refuses to admit it.

"Hey," Amelia nudges me, unknowingly hitting one of my newly acquired bruises. "Where's your head at?"

Trying not to wince, I reply, "Just thinking about my dad. Things aren't so great at home."

"I'm sorry, Randall. Is there anything I can do to help?" The sound of balls hitting pins is an odd backdrop for this conversation.

"Not really. I plan on talking to him this weekend."

"Randall, you're up," Jake hollers from the lane next to us, interrupting whatever Amelia was about to say.

Grabbing a bowling ball from the ball return, I toe the line at the lane. Not getting too close so the damn thing doesn't buzz. A couple of months ago, I would have thought all of us hanging out together was weird. Hell, I did think it was. Seeing how much both Tonya and Jake love Layla, I know them having a friendship makes everything easier. That little girl knows that both sets of parents love her fiercely.

The little girl in question toddles up to me. She points from the ball in my hand to the lane. I am assuming she wants to be a part of the action. "Hey, Layla, do you want to bowl for me?"

"Bowl," she yells and claps her hands excitedly. I don't see how she doesn't have every single person she meets wrapped around her tiny, little fingers. All it took was her pointing at my bowling ball for me to give in.

Amelia is already scooting the ball ramp kids use to the lane before I have a chance to ask for it. We don't have bumpers on either lane, so there's no telling where this ball may end up.

Placing the ball on the apparatus, I hold it in place with one hand while bending down and setting Layla on my knee with the other. "Are you ready, baby girl?"

She begins pushing on the ball and becomes frustrated when it won't budge. It's funny, and adorable, when she gets angry. I've seen her in full on temper tantrum so I'm not going to delay this too much longer. The next time she pushes on it, I push on it as well, releasing the ball down the ramp and making it's path along the lane. For a second, I think it's going to veer right and head straight to the gutter. But it doesn't, it rolls straight down the lane, knocking down all ten pins.

I stand up, adjusting Layla until she is sitting on my hip, and throw my arm up in victory. Just like that movie when the guy is walking across the football field. It really does feel exhilarating. "Layla, you are going to have to bowl for me more often. You are definitely my good luck charm." I tickle her side and she kicks her feet as she laughs. This time Amelia doesn't miss the jerk of pain when Layla accidentally hits one of my bruises.

When her eyebrows raise in question, I mouth "later." It seems to satisfy her for now. I know there will be a ton of questions as soon as we are alone. She's not going to like what I have to say.

Jake swoops in and pulls Layla from my arms. "Oh no, you are not allowed to bowl for Uncle Randall anymore. You need to pass all of that luck daddy's way. Then I can start making bets with all your other aunts and uncles, and win some money."

"Or," Tonya interjects. "You can all bowl for yourselves, and not rely on a one-year-old."

Reaf laughs, "She's just mad because she's losing."

"Keep laughing, and we'll see who's losing later." I can't tell if the smirk on Tonya's face is playful or evil, but it shuts Reaf up pretty quickly. A laugh bursts from my mouth without permission, and he glares at me.

"Oh, you just wait," he tells me. "There will be a time when Amelia will use your jokes against you. And on that day," he pauses for suspense. "I will be bent over, laughing my ass off at you."

Amelia smiles sweetly at me. She's not fooling me. Reaf forgets I grew up with her during the summers. She has a mean streak when she wants to. Even after her and Tonya would tell on us for picking on them, they would get their revenge.

There are only a couple of frames left in the game, and I can't wait to be out of this bowling alley. It hasn't changed one bit since we started coming here when we were in junior high. The plus side is it's not busy. We are literally the only group here. It's definitely not where I planned on spending my Monday night. It's where

Amelia was going to be, and I want to be wherever she is. Especially after the bullshit with my dad over the weekend.

Amelia saunters up to the lane and bends over, wiggling her butt before rolling the ball down the lane. She's doing it on purpose to distract me, and I will not let her win. Even if her ass looks great in those jeans.

"It's your turn," she places a quick peck on my cheek and sits down beside me.

She's two pins ahead of me. All I need is a spare to win. I glance at Layla, hoping they'll let me steal her for a second to help me bowl. The scowl on Tonya's face, makes the decision for me. I won't be getting any help from my good luck charm right now.

"You. Are. Going. Down." Picking my ball up, I reenact the butt wiggle Amelia just did. She laughs so loudly I almost drop the ball. My arm swings back, then forward, and I release the ball. Turning, I face Amelia, not watching how many pins I hit. A triumphant smile on my face.

It's not until I hear Jake mutter, "Damn, dude" that I turn around. The ball went into the freaking gutter. No way. How in the hell did I lose? It should have gone straight down the middle. It must have been me mocking her that threw me off my game. You know, karma, and all that crap.

"What was that you were saying?" Amelia teases. "I think I deserve ice cream after kicking your ass tonight."

I snort. "You act like you weren't going to get any ice cream anyway."

"But now," she bats her eyelashes at me. "It will be in celebration of my sweet, sweet victory."

"You tell him, sister," Tonya laughs. "Gotta train them early."

"I do what I do for you because I love you, woman," Reaf announces, loudly. "Not because I'm trained."

Tonya and Layla are standing side by side. Her arms loaded down with a diaper bag, her purse, and another bag that holds a few toys for Layla. Without a word, Reaf grabs all the bags from his wife's hands and heads outside to get the truck. Tonya scoops Layla into her arms and nods at us, knowingly. Amelia finds it funnier than I think she should, and she rolls her eyes. "That's called being a gentleman," she whispers to me.

Wiping my hand across my forehead in mock relief, I say, "Thank goodness you don't think I need to be trained."

"Nope," she giggles. "I like you just the way you are."

She's not going to like anything very much when I have to tell her about the bruises. "Are you ready to get out of here?"

"Absolutely." She slides her hand in mine, stands on her tiptoes and gives me a quick kiss.

I put my arm around her and pull her closer to me, trying to deepen the kiss. Amelia ducks out of my grasp and begins pulling me toward the car. Shit, this girl is on a mission, and I have a feeling it's going to revolve around me.

As soon as we're in the car, I put the key in the ignition and start it. Hand on the gear shift, I'm about to put it in reverse, but Amelia puts her hand over mine. "Wait."

"Can we talk about this later? We had a fun time in there, and I don't want to ruin with talks about my dad." Running my hand through my hair, I sigh.

"Nope." She crosses her arms over her chest. "We're going to talk about it now." She lifts my shirt up and gasps. "Did he do this to you?"

"It wasn't intentional," I confess. "He tried to hit me, lost his balance and started wildly swinging." Her knowing how horrible my dad can be is that last thing I want, but she deserves to know the shit show she is getting into by being with me. "I was trying to pin his arms to his sides, and he elbowed me by accident a few times. I'm fine though." Pressing lightly on my skin, I do my best to make her believe it. "It doesn't even hurt."

And it doesn't, not really. The physical things will heal. It's my mind that's a fucking a mess. The pain Mom caused when she left is still felt by both of us. I only wish he wouldn't continue to damage his health to numb his feelings. That lesson was learned back in high school. There is still a small part of me that's waiting for Amelia to bail on me, too. Keeping my guard partially up so I'm not destroyed when she decides she can't handle being with me. Or, I do something to inevitably screw up what we have.

"It doesn't matter if it hurts or not," Amelia protests. "He's your parent and shouldn't be laying hands on you. Period."

My eyes are focused on the steering wheel. I don't even have the guts to look at her. "Not everyone has the perfect family."

"This isn't about having a perfect, or imperfect, family, Randall. You really need to talk to your dad about his drinking problem." She's quiet for a few seconds. She's not done. "Or maybe you should move out of the house so you won't be exposed to his bad days."

"I can't do that, Amelia. He's my *father*. There isn't anyone around to take care of him besides me. If I leave, he won't be able to pay rent. Or worse, he'll do something stupid, and end up hurting himself. As much as I detest him most days, if anything happened, I would never forgive myself." That is the cold truth in all of this. I'm stuck. There is no other path for me. Not unless I can talk him into going to rehab. He's proud, though. The last time I brought up the possibility, he refused to admit he had a problem. That was the day I gave up any hope of having a normal life. Until *her*.

"Just promise you'll at least think about it if things get rougher than they are."

"I promise," I mumble while trying once again to put the car in reverse.

"Look me in the face and promise me, Randall," she raises her voice. "It doesn't count if I can't see your eyes."

Bringing my gaze to hers, I hold eye contact while

saying the words she wants to hear. "I promise I'll think about it." It's the first and only lie I'll tell her because no matter how bad it gets, I can't give up on the man that's raised me while trying to deal with his own heartbreak. Even if he is a selfish asshole for closing himself off completely.

"Good," she nods. "Now, let's go get my victory ice cream. Arguing with you is hard work."

"You're the boss," I grin. Grateful she's changed the subject, I finally reverse out of the parking lot, and turn onto the main road that runs through town. Getting her ice cream for kicking my ass is definitely a better way to end this night than arguing about my dad. I would do anything to keep her smiling the way she is right now.

amelia

"ARE you ready for book club tonight?" Tonya asks over the phone. It's my lunch break right now, and I would much rather be talking to Randall. It's not that I don't love my cousin, but I'm going to see her in a few hours. Randall and I haven't seen each other since we went bowling on Monday. I'd be lying if I said I didn't miss him. We are living in the same town, and we can't manage to find the time to hang out. Only talking over the phone is getting old.

Twirling my fork in my bowl of spaghetti, I sigh. "Sure. What are we going to do besides nerd out?"

"You don't sound very excited," Tonya mutters. "It's nothing crazy or super involved. All we do is sit around at Brew's Clues, and pretend to talk about a book none of us have read."

Dammit, I actually finished it. "So, if none of you have read the book, why have a book club?" The whole thing seems asinine. Normally, things like this wouldn't bother me. Except I actually took the time to read that book. It wasn't even something I would normally enjoy, and while I didn't love it, it didn't put me to sleep either. That's a plus because I'm really not a reader.

"It's just an excuse to leave the house and drink copious amounts of coffee without the other halves griping about being bored."

I stop spinning the fork in my hand. "Wait. All of this to get away from your husband?"

"Of course not," she laughs. "I love being around Reaf, but I also need to remember that I'm more than just a mom and wife. It's time carved out for *me*." She lets out a breath. "You'll understand when you are settled down. You're still in that new puppy love phase."

"I happen to like this stage. Thank you very much," I snap. "I'm sorry. You didn't deserve that. It's just I haven't even seen Randall since Monday, and I'm getting a little antsy. Since all the crap with Andrew, I second guess everything."

"Everything is fine," she reassures me. "Randall can be a pain in the ass sometimes. If there's anything I've learned about him in all the years I've known him, it's that he's incredibly loyal."

What she's telling me should make me feel better, but it doesn't stop the doubt from creeping in. From taking over every single thought that passes through my mind. "I'll take your word for it."

"You should," she says. "I've known him for pretty much my whole life. Even if I had my reservations about you being close to him in the beginning, I like seeing you happy. You're more *you* than you have been in months. It's a good change."

A quick glance at the clock on the wall, tells me I need to get back to work. "My lunch break is almost over. I should probably get off the phone so I can finish shoveling food in my mouth."

"Sounds good," she chirps. "Do you want me to pick you up, or are you going to meet us there?"

That's a good question. If I ride with Tonya, I'll be stuck there until she's ready to leave. If I drive myself I might be able to duck out early. "I'll meet you there. Do I need to even bother bringing the book I read for nothing?"

"I think it's only fair since, you know, I actually *read* it," I laugh. "I might even ask you guys questions about the book."

"If that's what you feel you need to do." My gut is telling me she just rolled her eyes at me. She's a smart ass when I can't even see her.

"Well, I have to go for real now. I'll see you later."

"Bye." She barely gets the word out before I'm hitting the end button.

Two minutes. That's all I have left in my break. I have two options... Eat as much of this spaghetti as fast as I can and risk making myself sick. Or, put it up and eat it when I get home.

The latter wins. There's nothing professional about a sales associate losing her lunch in front of customers.

* * *

Shit. I'm going to be late to "book club" tonight. The first few days, I was worried I wouldn't have enough things to do to keep me busy. As the days get longer, and warmer, more people visit the shop. Most are looking for clothing to take on beach vacations. Some are moms looking for the perfect outfits for their little girls. Something they can wear to backyard barbecues that are cute but still functional.

That is the biggest difference I've seen in the two shops I've now worked at. The one back home had beautiful clothes for all ages, but most of them came with special cleaning instructions. Here, almost everything can be done with regular laundry. There's no need to send it out for dry cleaning. It's something I think the customers really appreciate. It doesn't add more to their already full plates.

Now, if I could get these customers out of the door, that would be great. This lady came in ten minutes before we were supposed to close, and she's *still* here. The shop closed twenty minutes ago. If I didn't know how much customer satisfaction meant to my boss, I'd have told her to come back tomorrow. In a town this small, something like that would bring bad PR to the store, and I can't have that.

"Ma'am," I say just above a whisper to keep from startling her. "Is there anything I can help you with?" Because this isn't the millionth time I've asked her since she's been here. A wide smile is plastered to my face. In my head, I'm shoving her out the door and running in the opposite direction.

"Actually," she says, back straight. "You may be able to. I need a Fourth of July dress for my granddaughter."

"Do you know what size she wears?" That would make the process a hell of a lot easier on me.

"No, she's a little over a year old." She shrugs. It looks odd on this woman who carries herself as if she's the most important person in town. "Maybe that will help on the sizing."

Leading her to the wall of themed dresses, I pull out one sized at eighteen months and another that's a 2T. The material is stretchy so it should fit either way. "We have these." I hold them up in the air, doing my best to show them off without being off putting.

"Are those the only ones you have?"

"Yes," I nod. "We haven't gotten the rest of our summer stock yet. You can come back in a few weeks, if you'd like to look at the full selection."

She clasps her hands together, weighing her decision. "That may be the best thing to do. It will give me a chance to ask what size she wears. Until then, can you hold these for me?"

"Absolutely." Setting the dresses behind the counter, I make a note to hold until the rest of the collection comes in. "Can I get your name to ensure nobody grabs these?"

"Yes," she huffs. She acts like I'm supposed to know who she is. "It's Diane."

My eyes go wide when she mentions her name. Doing my best to school my features into a blank mask, I turn. "There we go. It shouldn't be more than two weeks before we have the new merchandise in."

There's no goodbye, or thanking me for keeping the shop open much later than usual, to accommodate her. Good riddance.

At least I'll have some juicy information to bring to the table when I make it to the coffee shop. Tonya is going to lose her shit.

And so much for eating my lunch for dinner. It's a good thing they have pastries at the coffee shop, or I might starve until I make it home later tonight.

* * *

"Absolutely not," Tonya shrieks. "You will not, under any circumstances, sell that woman a dress for my child."

That's exactly the reaction I knew she would have. Not that I blame her. Everything I've heard about Jake's parents has been awful. They sound like miserable people who want to control everyone.

"I second that," Charleigh says from the big red couch next to Tonya. Some days it's weird to me that the two of them hang out, but I'm happy they don't fight like most people who share a child. "That woman is unhinged," she shudders. "I've only had the *pleasure* of meeting her twice, and that was two times too many."

"Maybe she'll forget, and won't come back," I say, trying to calm my cousin down. "That's probably the best-case scenario for everyone involved. I mean who exactly is she going to ask for Layla's size? It's not like you're going to hand that information over freely. And, I'm pretty sure Jake isn't talking to them."

"He's not," Charleigh chimes in.

Taking a sip of coffee, Tonya thinks over what I said. "You're right. Hopefully she forgets." She takes another sip, "Besides, she will probably go somewhere else since your store didn't have anything she liked. If there's one thing I know about that woman it's that she's impatient."

"So, Charleigh," I change the subject. If I don't Tonya is going to stew on it for days. "Did you read the book we're *supposed* to be discussing?"

She shoots a panicked look toward Tonya. "Um," she begins, but doesn't get a chance to finish.

Bianca's voice comes from behind me, "They never do. I've been reading them in hopes that one day they'll actually talk about the books we pick out." She shakes her head in disappointment, "They are missing out on some pretty amazing books."

"I thought you had to work tonight," Charleigh says.

"Eh," Bianca shrugs. "We were slow so I cut out early.

There's no point in me being there if nobody is coming in. Weeknights are always slow, anyway."

The only ones missing from the group are Cami and Darcy, They'll be back soon enough. Once finals are done, they'll be heading back home with their boyfriends in tow. We're an odd group combination, and that only makes things more interesting. Especially when we try to explain to strangers how we've all become friends.

Tonya, Charleigh, and Bianca are talking about some cute thing Layla did. Tonya wants this time to be herself, but she can't stop talking about the little light of her life. Not that I blame her. Layla is the cutest, and funniest, baby I've ever encountered. She already has an amazing personality, and I can't wait to see what she does in life.

As much as I love my baby cousin, the conversation is kind of boring. My thoughts drift to Randall, and I wonder what he's doing right now. He had to work, and he should be getting off soon. He'll probably go hang out with Jake and Marshall since I'm not free tonight. The urge to bail on this "book club" is strong. The only thing holding me back is myself. In a good way, of course. When I dated Andrew, I was with him all the time. He wanted to be around me as much as I did him, or so I thought. And even though I *really* like Randall, I don't want to become so attached to him that I lose myself. Being so dependent on someone only to have them shatter me, was one of the worst things I've experienced, and I won't go through that again. Space is definitely a good thing.

"Earth to Melly," Tonya snaps her fingers in front of my face. "Girl, you zoned out for a hot minute. Are you okay?"

"Oh, um, yeah. I'm fine," I mutter. Glancing at the clock I realize I've been going over my relationship with Randall for over ten minutes.

"I bet I can guess where your mind was," Tonya smirks.

"I knew you two were going to get together," Charleigh squeals. "I could see it in your mannerisms. Even without the almost kiss in Bianca's work room."

"In my what?" Bianca screeches.

"Nothing happened," I roll my eyes. "We were waiting on Charleigh to draw up my tattoo, and were talking." I motion toward Charleigh. "She walked in when I was about to kiss him. I was so freaking embarrassed."

Bianca isn't scowling anymore. Her hands are covering her mouth trying to hold her giggles in. "If you only knew what has happened in that room," she winks.

"Gross," the rest of us say in unison. "That was something I could have gone my whole life without hearing," I laugh. "And I'll never go in there again."

"Whatever," Bianca huffs. "I sanitize if every morning, night, and after each client. That's probably one of the cleanest rooms in the whole shop."

"Speaking of," I take a bite of my muffin. "What's going on with your receptionist? Randall mentioned something about a crush on one of the other artists."

"Yeah, that's Sophie," Charleigh answers. "She's had a crush on Adrian since she started working there. He's going through a lot right now. They are both ridiculously hot for each other. Neither of them will do anything about it, though"

"It's painful to watch," Bianca says. "They definitely need to figure their shit out." She pauses for a second and her eyes light up. I swear, if it was possible, there would be a bright light bulb above her head. "Maybe we should invite her to hang out with us. I don't think she has very many friends. She's nice and doesn't cause drama. What do y'all think?"

"I'm okay with it." It's not like my input really matters since I'm just now joining the group, but it would be nice to have another newbie around. We're really turning into a family of misfits. It reminds me of that old Christmas movie with the elf that wants to be a dentist.

Tonya and Charleigh nod in agreement. Sometimes I think my cousin thrives on including people. It's like we're all lost puppies and she's trying to give us a home, one stray at a time. Between her and Randall, the decision to go back home once I'm on my feet is becoming more difficult. Here, I have friends, a boyfriend, and a job I really enjoy. All I have back at home are a job and my parents. Not that my parents are a bad thing. They've been nothing but supportive of me and my decisions. I just need, and want, something else. Something more. It might be time for me to plant my roots in a new location for a bit.

Tonya's phone dings, and we all look at her. "It's probably just Reaf. Let me check really quick just in case something's wrong with Layla." Seconds later she's laughing so hard she almost knocks over her cup of coffee.

"What did he say?" I ask. Anything that creates that sort of laughter has to be funny.

"He's cursing me for having to change a poopy diaper." She has another fit of laughter. "As if I haven't done it five million times."

"Men," Charleigh shakes her head.

There's not really much to say after that. Though, I can only imagine how Reaf feels about it. Anytime I'm with Layla and she has a dirty diaper, I take her straight to her mama. It's also the reason I never keep her when I'm by myself.

The employees of Brew's Clues begin shutting off the coffee machines, our cue to get out. Time has flown hanging out with them, and I'm happy they invited me. Even if I didn't want to come to begin with.

"I think we better get out of here before they officially kick us out," Charleigh notices the shut down routine.

"Okay, ladies," Tonya claps her hands. "We'll figure out a time for next month. Until then, I have to go make sure my husband isn't drowning our apartment with Febreze.

The entire drive home my thoughts are whirling so

quickly, I can barely keep up. Note to self, coffee at night probably isn't the best idea. Tea may be better next time. The one thing I keep focusing on is the question Randall asked me the first time we went to the park. What do I want for myself?

Working in the boutique brings me so much joy, but I don't want to be a retail worker for the rest of my life. It wouldn't be so horrible to maybe own a store one day, though. It's something I'll have to think about more. Everything in my life is starting to look up after the months of sinking into myself. Maybe it's possible to have everything I want, Randall included, without any of the heartache.

randall

SUMMER IS ALREADY HITTING us full force. The days are long and stifling with heat. Not exactly the best time for the air conditioner in my car to die. I should have seen it coming. This car has been nothing but problematic the past few weeks. And, of course, it would happen when I'm supposed to take Amelia out.

The past month and a half with her has been amazing. We've been inseparable, well except for nights when we're both working or when she has that book club with the girls. After the book meeting last month, she complained about not actually talking about the book. Then talked about how much fun she had and couldn't wait to do it again. Girls can be so weird sometimes.

Opening up my text messages, I send one to Amelia.

. . .

Randall: Would you despise not having a/c on the way to our date tonight?

Amelia: Uh-oh. What happened?

It's so embarrassing that I even need to have this conversation. If my life had taken a different path, or my dad didn't drown in his own pool of self-loathing, I could be driving a decent car. Not something that I hope gets me to where I need to be. One day I'll have the car I need.

Randall: It's not working in my car.

Amelia: Weren't we going to the drive-in anyway? I'll just put my hair up and we can put the windows down.

Randall: Are you sure?

Amelia: Duh. It's not like I'm super high maintenance or anything.

Randall: Okay, cool. I'll pick you up in a few hours. Have a great rest of your day.

Amelia: You too. :)

This is why I'm slowly falling in love with this woman. She doesn't care about appearances or anything like that. With her, actions are what speak the loudest. I plan on doing everything I can to show her how much I care about her, and maybe she won't go back home. Maybe I'll be enough of a reason for her to stay.

Dad stumbles into the house. The talk we had a few weeks ago did absolutely nothing. He's still getting shit-face drunk and being a complete asshole. He did listen to me, though. Catching him at a time when he doesn't have a beer in his hand isn't easy. He made promises that he's already broken many times over, and I'm starting to lose all faith in him. He doesn't *want* to give up drinking, and until that happens... I'm wasting my breath. It's going to take him hitting rock bottom before that happens.

"Randall," he shouts. "Get in here, son."

Absolutely anything else sounds better than facing whatever he's going to yell about. Hell, I'd willingly spend time with Jake's parents to evade my father. But I move my feet toward the living room. Stalling will only piss him off more.

"Hey, Dad." My voice is light, hiding the tension behind it. "What's up?"

"Why are you home?"

"Today is my day off," I reply, worried this is going to be another time I have to pin him down. "But I'll be heading out in an hour or so."

He doesn't say anything. Lifting the can of beer to his lips, he shakes his head, then takes a long swig. "That girl is going to let you down, just like *she* did."

It's an argument we've had numerous times since he found out I was dating Amelia. Apparently, I'm supposed to stay single forever and clean up his messes. "Maybe," I shrug. "At least I'm trying to have a normal relationship instead of living in the past. By the way, I gave the landlord the money for rent. We have a place to live for another month."

This time I don't wait for a response. I go to my room, grab my wallet and keys, and walk out the back door. If he wants to stew on a past, he can't change, he can do it alone. I'm not going to argue with him about my life when he refuses to actually *live* his own. Besides, I need to go to the store anyway. A picnic at the drive-in is exactly what I need tonight. Being with one of the most amazing people I know doesn't hurt either.

"You didn't need to go through all this trouble," Amelia gasps when I let her know she can come out of the car. I made her wait until I had the blanket and food spread out like a feast.

My cheeks warm. "I know that. I wanted to. And, it's a beautiful night. Why waste that on concession stand food and sitting in a hot car." Truth be told, it's hot as hell tonight. Sitting in the car would be stifling and uncomfortable. Having my ass stick to the seat from sweat isn't my idea of a good time. Not to mention trying to hold her hand when mine is damp and gross. That can't be attractive to ladies.

"Who knew you were such a romantic?" She clasps her hands together and sighs. She looks like one of the girls that fawn over Gaston anytime they are in his presence. It would be annoying if it wasn't so cute. This girl could do anything and I would find it adorable. I am definitely falling for her more and more every minute I spend with her.

"It's not a huge deal," I whisper. She knows my money situation and where it all goes. I can't afford to take her to do things most boyfriends would. Her being appreciative of the small things I can offer means more to me than anything else.

"And," she kisses my cheek. "That's my favorite part. You don't try to impress me with frivolous things I don't care about." She leans her head on my shoulder. "Remember, I'm not high maintenance. I'm good with keeping things mellow."

Right as I'm turning to kiss her the way I want to, the movie starts, and her focus is on the massive screen sitting in the middle of a field. Sounds of families, and couples drift toward us almost drowning out the previews coming from the crackling speakers next to the cars. The conversations from Mom and Dad about how they used to come to a place just like this every weekend enter my thoughts. Even though, Mom didn't want us, *me*, anymore, I'm filled with peace knowing they were happy... at least for a little while.

Instead of spending time thinking about a family that no longer exists, I cherish the time I have with the girl by my side. You never know when the most important people in your life will leave without a moment's notice.

* * *

It's around midnight when the movies end, and it's time for us to leave the drive-in. Getting out of here is almost as bad as it is to get out of football games. The line of cars trying to be the first to get out is ridiculous. Things would go a lot smoother if they would just let every other car in the line.

We don't make a move to the car just yet, though. We'll let these crazies jam the entrance until there is almost nobody left. We lie back on the blanket and admire the stars. "It still baffles me that you can see the stars so well out here."

"Why? Do you not have the same sky at home?"

She scoots closer to me despite the heat. Not caring if we get sweat on each other. "We do. There's even a great place to stargaze at my parent's house. I've just never taken the time to do it."

Amelia referring to her house as her parent's doesn't slip my notice. That may be a sign that she's planning to stick around for a while. She hasn't mentioned anything, but I'm holding out hope. Her being here for the long haul would help ease the fear I have of her up and leaving me. Most would say it's an irrational fear. Those people have clearly never been left behind and unwanted.

"What are you thinking about?" Amelia says into my neck.

There's no way I'm going to tell her I'm obsessing

154

over something that may not happen. "How perfect this night has been." It's not a lie. Not completely, anyway. "There wasn't any drama or the whole group of us being loud and crazy."

"Oh yeah," she says, excitedly. "Don't forget we're supposed to go to the lake with everyone tomorrow."

"I can't wait." This isn't a lie either. The lake is one of my happy places. It's away from my dad, and we can fish, swim, and cookout without having anything to worry about. "The traffic has died down. Let's get out of here. We're going to need as much sleep as possible. This crew doesn't just go to the lake for a few hours. We spend the entire day on the water."

Sitting up, I pull her next to me. I don't let her go. Within seconds she's in my lap, legs straddling my hips. If we were anywhere else, I'd find this sexy as hell. We're in public, though, and I have to do my best to tamp down my hormones. It's not easy. "I thought we were going?" She whispers in my ear.

Dammit. Amelia is making this incredibly hard. I want to forget that we're not alone more than anything. A groan escapes my lips, "We are. I just wanted to hold you for a little bit."

With every kiss I press against her neck, she scoots closer. Testing my willpower further. Wrapping my arms around her, I bring her even closer, and lean in to kiss her. She throws her arms around my neck, and deepens the kiss. She's at an advantage since she's a smidge taller than me while sitting on my lap.

I'm lost in her, the way she tastes, and how her lips feel pressed against mine. It's the sweetest torture not being able to go any further. "Hey, the lot has emptied out. It's time for you to leave," a deep voice calls from the darkness. It's like cold water being splashed on us, breaking the spell we are under.

"Crap," she mutters into my hair. "We should probably go before they call the cops or something."

"They won't do that," I chuckle. "The worst that would happen is being banned from this place."

We stand up, and begin cleaning our area. We don't want to leave any sort of mess after being reprimanded for fooling around after closing. Maybe we can sneak away while we're at the lake tomorrow. The likelihood is slim, but a guy can dream. For now, I'll get her home before her aunt and uncle start blowing up her phone.

I'm out of the house before Dad even wakes up. He must have passed out in his room last night because I didn't see him when I came home either. It's one less fight I'll have to endure, and I'm not complaining. One small victory for the day.

The roads are empty this early in the morning. Amelia doesn't do well with mornings and I can't help but wonder what sort of mood she's going to be in. Hopefully it's nothing like Cami. I don't plan on talking to her until after lunch if I can help it. If everyone else is smart, they won't either.

Brew's Clue is open and empty. While everyone else in town is catching up on their beauty sleep on this already scorching Saturday, I'm getting my girl the biggest cup of coffee this place has to offer. It's the least I can do for making her get up so early on a weekend that she doesn't have to work. She could have said no when I invited her. Not that her cousin would have allowed that answer. Even though she's been getting out more than she did a few months ago, they keep harping on her about getting out more. One day she's going to lose it on her family for being so meddlesome.

Before getting out of the car, I reach into the cup holder for my wallet. Except... it's not there. I could have sworn I left it in here last night out of fear I'd forget it this morning. I guess I won't be showing up on Amelia's doorstep with the caffeine I know she'll want so badly.

A quick glance at my watch tells me I'm already late to pick her up. Shit. We'll have to stop by my house on the way to the lake. There's a chain coffee shop on the way for us to stop by. If all is right with the world, my dad will still be asleep.

She's already waiting outside when I pull up to the house, sitting on a big red and white ice chest.

"How are you going to tell me to be ready at this God awful hour, then show up late?" She scolds me before I even have the door halfway open.

"Well," I smile. "I was trying to be a good boyfriend and get you coffee before picking you up."

She searches my hands then jumps up looking in the car. "Where is it?" Her desperation for that first sip of energy would be funny if she didn't look quite so upset about the lack of coffee.

"I didn't have my wallet on me." Grabbing the ice chest, I carry it to my car. Amelia is already sitting in the passenger seat while I hoist the heavy box into the backseat. "What do you have in this thing?"

"Aunt Lucia loaded it up with food and water." She gives me a questioning look. "Are we going by your house?"

The reluctance in her voice kills me. Especially since I'm the one who told her how awful he is most of the time. He has good days. They are just few and far between. "Yeah," I answer. "You can stay in the car, though. It will only take me a second to run in and get it."

"That's probably a good idea," she mutters. "One day I want to meet your dad, but not until he starts living for *you* and not *himself*."

I give her hand a quick squeeze. She's always looking out for what's best for me. Being cared about, and for, hasn't happened in so long. I almost forgot what it feels like.

Amelia dozes off on the drive to my house. As soon as her eyes drifted shut, I turned the radio down. Not wanting to bother her.

Now we're in my driveway, and I don't know if I should wake her, or let her sleep. The latter wins. Pulling on the handle, I open the door as quietly as possible, and leave it open after getting out.

Dad's truck is still here, except I don't hear any noise coming from inside. Fingers crossed he's still asleep, I open the front door. Fate is a fickle bitch because my dad is standing in the hallway with my wallet in his hand. "Forget something?"

amelia

MY EYES SLOWLY OPEN. Crap, I didn't mean to fall asleep on the poor guy. Turning to my left, I realize he's not in the car and the driver side door is wide open. Where did he go?

It's only then I begin to take in my surroundings. The house is white, or at least it used to be. Paint is chipping off in big chunks. The front porch is sagging as if it can no longer bear the weight it's been given. The blinds covering the windows have gaping holes in them rendering them almost useless. This must be Randall's house.

The outward appearance isn't what has me getting out of the car, rushing toward it. It's the shouting coming from inside. His dad must be giving him a hard time. Running in there probably isn't a smart idea given everything Randall has told me about the person that was tasked with raising him. I can't just sit in the car and act like there isn't a huge fight going on inside those walls.

I'm a few yards from the house when I hear Randall yell, "Give me my fucking wallet, Dad."

Stopping in my tracks, I'm not so sure I want to go in there anymore. Fear for Randall propelled me here, but I've never been in this sort of situation. Arguing parents is normal, just not at this level. I can't think of a time I would ever speak to my mom or dad the way Randall just spoke to his. It makes me wonder if this is what he's capable of when his temper gets the best of it. Even though I've never seen him truly get angry, that doesn't mean he's not capable of it. He has enough torment stored up inside him to fuel it.

Randall storms out of the front door, wallet in hand. "Let's go."

An older man follows him out. His hair is graying and he looks like he hasn't shaved in about a week. He looks much older than he probably is thanks to the lifestyle he's led since his wife left him. "She's going to leave you just like your mom did," he slurs. "I don't know why the hell you're spending money on her when it's not going to last."

"I said let's go," Randall grabs my hand, pulling me toward the car.

"That's right, run away," his dad laughs. "Just don't come crying to me when she decides she doesn't want you anymore. When she breaks your heart and destroys you."

Randall drops my hand and spins around. "Like you have room to talk. What the hell do you think you've been doing the past fourteen years," he shouts. "I've had to raise myself, or rely on my friends' parents. *I'm* the one who has been paying the rent since I was able to work. And what exactly have you done?" He taps his fingers on his chin. "Oh, that's right. You stay drunk all the time, floating from job to job because you can't even show up to work *sober*."

"You little shit," his dad spits out. "If you think you're so grown, come at me like a real man."

Randall doesn't hesitate. He closes the distance between him and his father, and raises his arm. Readying for a punch. It's a good thing I followed close behind him, even though every cell in my body was telling me to stay back. Grabbing his arm, I try to hold him back with all the strength I possess. "Don't do this, Randall," I whisper, harshly. "You'll regret it later."

He shrugs me off, takes a step back, and shakes his head. "Let's get out of here." He waits until I start walking to car before following me. His dad glaring daggers at him the entire time.

Anger radiates off of him, yet he still manages to take the time to open the door for me. Showing me that none of this is directed toward me. As soon as I'm safely tucked away in the car, he gives his dad one last look and gets in the car. Putting the car in reverse, the tires spin as he backs out of the driveway.

Both of us are silent as he drives as fast as he can

away from his house. The only place he's called home despite the bullshit he has to deal with. Minutes pass before he pulls over, puts the car in park, and leans his head against the steering wheel.

He doesn't say anything for a while, gathering his composure. Finally, he turns his head until he's facing me. "I'm so fucking sorry, Amelia. I never meant for you to see that. To see *him*."

"It's not your fault," I reach over, placing my hand on his leg. "You can't control his actions. One day he'll regret the way he's treated you."

"The way I acted wasn't any better," he sniffles, a tear sliding down his cheek. If I wasn't terrified of his dad, I'd march my ass back to the house and tell him exactly what I think. "And, for that, I apologize." Slipping his hand over mine, he gives it a gentle squeeze. "You know I'd never hurt you, right?"

I nod. His actions did scare me, though. Deep down, I know he's never done anything to put me in harms' way, at least not intentionally. His father knows how to push his buttons. He can't avoid him forever since they live in the same house. Even with what went down a few minutes ago, it's not enough for me to abandon him. I will not be something to be used against him out of fear.

"I'm sure everyone is wondering where we are," his says as he straightens up. "We should probably get to the lake."

Any hope I had of things going back to the playful vibe we had when he picked me up are gone when he turns the radio up. It's not overly loud, but enough that I would have to raise my voice to be heard. Something in him changed back there, and I fear it will ruin us.

* * *

He was right. Everyone else in the group is already there. Ice chests, lawn chairs, and floats are scattered around a small section of the beach area. Layla is walking around with a life vest on. The thing looks like it's swallowing her. It can't be comfortable, but I'm happy Tonya is making her wear it. You can never be too careful, even when there are several pairs of eyes around to keep an eye on her.

"You're finally here," Tonya yells as we get out of the car. She scans me from head to toe. Taking in my jean shorts and t-shirt. "Please tell me you brought a bathing suit. There's no way you're going to be comfortable swimming in *that*."

"Who said I was going to swim?" Lifting my bag out of the car, I almost drop it. It may be little but I have a ton of crap shoved in there. "Do you have any idea how gross lake water is? You can't even see your feet a couple of feet in. And what if a fish touches me?" I shudder in mock disgust.

"You are so full of it," Tonya laughs. Of course, she would call me on my bullshit. We've grown up swimming in lakes. If Dad heard me make those comments, he'd throw me in just to prove a point. It's a good thing he's not here because my phone is in my back pocket, and that would be an expensive replacement.

I shrug. "You shouldn't ask stupid questions. My bathing suit is on under my clothes." I shift the top of my shorts down so she can see the red and white striped bikini bottoms. The guys start whistling, and laughing. "Oh my gosh. Grow up," I roll my eyes.

Randall stands beside me with the ice chest in his hands. "I'm going to set this down and go talk with the guys. You good?"

"Yeah," I reply with a sad smile. There's already a difference in him. He's the one that's terrified of being abandoned, and I can already feel him distancing himself from me. As if he's scared he's going to inadvertently lose, or hurt, me by bringing me further into his life.

With a quick peck on the cheek, he's takes off toward the group of guys forming a wall between Layla and the water. It's pretty effective from what I can see. They move in whichever direction she tries to run in. It's like watching a school of fish dart through the water. Synchronized motions to ward off any threats.

Walking down the small slope, I almost slip and fall. "Have you been drinking?" Cami calls out. "Isn't it a little early for that?"

"No, I haven't been drinking, asshole." I say just loud enough for them to hear.

"Language, cuz," Tonya admonishes me.

"Sorry," I mutter and toss my bag next to all their stuff.

Right now, I should be getting ready to jump in the lake and relax with my friends. Instead, I'm casting worried glances at Randall, trying to figure out where his head is at.

"What's the matter?" Charleigh places a hand on my shoulder. "Did something happen?"

Should I tell them? A part of me feels like maybe it's Randall's story to tell. Though, most of them probably already know the crap he has to deal with on a daily basis. Another part of me feels like it's okay for me to share what happened. I mean, I was there, and *witnessed* it. Randall is a much stronger person than I am because I would have already been gone from that hell hole. Of course, it's easy for me to say that because he's not my parent. If the roles were reversed, I'm sure I would feel guilty for wanting to get out.

"Hello," Tonya snaps. "You never answered the question.

"Sorry," I mumble. Taking a deep breath, I fill them in on the events of my morning. When I'm finished, I sneak a glance at Randall. He's laughing, and almost looks like his normal self. I see the way his shoulders are tight, and how rigidly he's standing. He's wearing the same mask he used to. He's indifferent, the way he was when we first started hanging out.

"I'm so sorry, girl," Darcy says. "That had to have been tough."

"It was, but it's nothing compared to the crap he goes through every day." Reaching into the ice chest, I grab a bottle of water. The ice feels amazing against my fevered skin. Sweating while standing still should not be possible, yet it is. "The only thing that worries me is he hasn't said anything since we left his dad's. Not really anyway. Is that healthy?"

Layla is running toward Tonya, well as fast as one-year old's can run, and within seconds she's in her arms. Watching my cousin try to balance Layla in her life jacket may be one of the funniest things I've seen all week. If only there were a way I could turn the whole ordeal into a meme. "Well," she says after getting Layla situated on her hip. "Probably not." She sighs, loudly. "Randall's never been one to talk about his feelings. He keeps everything bottled up until it just bursts."

"What do you mean by that?" I ask. My gut says he'd never lose his temper toward me. How well do I really know him? My biggest worry is that it'll end up being another situation similar to what I went through with Andrew. Then I'll be the one broken-hearted... Again.

Cami rushes to Tonya's defense. "Oh no, nothing physical. He'll get really mad and stalk off." She shrugs. "Most of the time. He's gotten into it with Jake a few times, but they treat all situations as if they are siblings, you know."

I don't know, not really. The closest thing I have to a sibling is Tonya. We were born months apart from each other and we've always stuck together. We've fought, of course, but the arguments never lasted long. Okay, so maybe I do understand. At least a little bit.

"I guess," I pause to take a drink. "It'd be a lot better if he'd just open up to me and let me know what's going on in that head of his."

"Girl," Tonya laughs. "That's never going to happen. Guys are so weird."

Charleigh claps her hands together. "Let's make it a good day and go jump in the lake."

Tonya sets Layla back down and grabs her hand. "Let's do this Bean."

Shaking my head, I follow behind them. Her nickname for her daughter is just as ridiculous as *Melly*. Today I'm going to enjoy myself as much as I can. Randall and I can talk later today, or even tomorrow. There's no need worrying about something I can't fix.

randall

"SO," Jake elbows me. "What are you going to do about your old man?"

They figured out the cause of my bad mood as soon as I got here. There's only one person who can fill me with that much rage. Derrick, Travis, and Reaf were the only ones that didn't know what was happening. Jake filled them in while I was watching Amelia.

I feel bad for ditching her the minute we got here. But I don't want her seeing me this frustrated. She's pulling her shirt and shorts off, revealing the small bikini underneath. It leaves all her curves on full display. Maybe I should go over and talk to her.

"I don't know what I'm going to do about him," I shrug. "There isn't much to do. He can't take care of himself, and I can't just leave him to suffer. Mom leaving all those years ago really fucked him up."

"He isn't your responsibility, Randall." This time

Marshall joins the conversation. "He's a grown man and needs to learn how to take care of himself."

"That's shocking coming from you," I snort. "You're always so hell bent on keeping the peace."

"Eh, your dad's an asshole." He points toward Jake. "Both of your parents should form a club exclusively for asshole parents."

Jake laughs. "You honestly think that would go over well. Hell, my mom's trying to buy clothes for a granddaughter she's never even met."

Everyone else's parents are normal compared to ours. Most want what's best for their kids, and want them to be happy. Mine and Jake's parents seem to have a competition on who can destroy their kids' lives the fastest. Jake walked away from his family and never looked back. I'm struggling to make the same choice.

"Well, as awesome as it is to talk about the shitty people that raised us," I point toward the girls getting in the water. "I'm going to see my girl for a bit."

The words my dad yelled keep replaying in my head. I *can't* believe that he's right. That she'll just leave me without a moment's notice. Pushing those thoughts away, I wade into the water until I'm right behind her.

"Hey." I wrap my hands around her waist. The subtle flinch shoots a pang straight to my heart. "Need some help."

She's trying to get on a float, but the waves coming from the jet skis further out are making it almost impossible. "Sure," she nods. "Can you hold this stupid thing still?"

"No problem." I grab the float and try to keep it as motionless as possible with the waves coming in. "Are you having fun?" The need to make some sort of conversation is overwhelming. We've never been stagnant around each other. Not even when we were just "friends."

Amelia gets on the float with no issue since I'm holding it in place for her. Once she's situated, she shade's her eyes from the sun. "Oh, so you're talking to me now?"

"I never wasn't talking to you," I argue. "I just needed to cool off for a bit."

"You know we're going to have to talk about what happened earlier, right?" She sighs, "That was pretty huge, and you shutting me out isn't the best thing in the world."

"I'm sorry," I run my hand through my hair. "Can we talk about it later? I'd rather not have an audience."

"Okay," she relents. "Don't think I'm going to forget about it though."

Honestly, I'm surprised she's not pressing me to talk about it now. She isn't one to let things go for long. When we first started talking, maybe. But now... She's like a dog with a bone. Not giving up until she gets what she wants.

"Have you ever been fishing?" Yes, I'm changing the subject, and I'm not ashamed to admit that I am.

"Yep," she smiles. "I used to go with my dad all the time. He doesn't understand why I like selling cute things you can't find in chain stores, so we bond by going fishing."

"You might be the only girl I know that actually likes fishing." How has this never come up in conversation before? It's one of my favorite hobbies, especially when I'm trying to get over whatever bullshit my dad has spouted off.

"Well, I'm also a little competitive about it." She's laughing. "My dad always tries to catch more than I do, but it rarely happens. Winner always gets to choose dinner."

Her close relationship with her parents makes me long for it. It will never happen, though a guy can wish. "I'll have to take you to my fishing spot one day. We'll see who catches the most."

"You're on," she swats me in the shoulder, almost falling off the float she's lying on. "Oh, are you coming to the Fourth of July party my aunt and uncle are having next weekend?"

"Only if you're inviting me," I say. "I haven't been to one since the summer before my junior year in high school."

"You say that like you're ancient or something," she snorts. "We're barely twenty."

"Some days it feels like it," I shrug. And it does. Having to be the parent to my dad is such a pain in the ass. There are times where I get home exhausted, and world weary, that I collapse into bed and fall asleep before I realize it.

"You're so dramatic." Water splashes me in the face. I didn't even realize her hand was in the water, waiting for the perfect opportunity.

"Oh, I'm dramatic, am I?" A smirk forms on my lips.

"No, Randall," she shrieks. "Whatever you're about to do, don't do it."

She doesn't have another opportunity to plead her case. I put both of my hands under the float and lift. Her arms fly up as she falls into the water. She's sputtering and swiping her hair from her face when she resurfaces, glaring at me.

"You looked like you needed to cool down," I chuckle.

"You're such a jachkole," she mutters. "I'm going to go over there," she motions toward Tonya and Cami. "They'll at least be nice to me."

She grabs her float, sticks her tongue out at me, and wades through the water until she's joined her cousin at the other end of the swimming area. She picks Layla up and bounces her in the water, making silly faces at her until the little girl's laughter fills the air. Even when she's angry at me, I'm attracted to her.

"Well, bud," Marshall slaps his hand on my shoulder. "Looks like you're stuck with us again."

"Unfortunately," I laugh. "Or, we can terrorize the girls."

"I would," he says. "Bianca can, and would, kick my ass. So, I'm out."

I splash water in his face. "That girl has you so wrapped around her finger, you don't know up from down."

"Like you're one to talk." He tackles me, forcing me to go under water. I don't go alone, I pull his arm so he goes down, too. Being with Amelia, and my friends, is freeing. Today feels the same way it did when we were kids. We're enjoying life, and all the things it has to offer us.

* * *

Amelia doesn't waste time as soon as we're back in the car, driving home from the lake. "So, let's talk."

Groaning, I turn the radio down. With those three words, she's brought down the great mood I was in. "What do you want to talk about?"

The sun is setting in the distance, but I can see the scowl on her face. "You know exactly what I want to talk about. You can't keep living like that. Always hoping you won't confront your dad, and being stuck in a hostile situation when you have to."

"I can't just leave either," I bite back. "He doesn't have anyone else."

"It's not fair to you, though." She covers my hand with her own. "I care about you Randall, and I want what's best for you." She's silent for a bit, gathering her thoughts, determining the best way to put them into words. "You remember the first night we went to the park?"

"Yeah," I sigh. "Why?"

"You asked me what I wanted out of life. At the time I didn't know. I know what I want now. To own my own boutique and you."

"Does that mean you aren't leaving?"

"No, I'm not," she squeezes my hand. "You also need to take the steps to get what you want out of life. Sitting stagnant in your childhood home isn't going to get you anywhere."

We're on her street now, and as much as I don't want my evening with her to end, I don't want to talk about all of this. "I'll think about it." The words aren't to placate her. I will think about it, but not tonight.

Once the car is in park, she leans over and gives me a quick kiss. "You should probably get some rest. I know you have to open the store tomorrow."

Pulling her closer to me, I press my lips to hers. Deepening it with every passing second. Moments like this are the highlights of my days. It's what gives me hope for a better tomorrow. These small pockets of time when the world is quiet, I'm not over thinking anything, and the girl I'm head over heels for is in my arms. She pulls away with a happy sigh. "Text me when you get home."

"I'll see you at the party," I call out the open window. My work schedule this week is intense, and I won't have a ton of free time to see Amelia.

"You better," she smiles.

After making sure she makes it in the house safely, I back out of the driveway. She has a point with what she said about staying at home. My dad needs me, though. He doesn't realize it now, and I hope one day he will. I just can't leave him when he's such a mess. Knowing what it feels like to have nobody looking out for you, I can't put that emotion on him. Even if he deserves it.

My biggest fear is Amelia will start to pull away if I don't make a change. She took the fight with my dad this morning in stride. She had to have been shaken up afterward, but she didn't let on that anything was amiss. I don't want my life to become her new normal. She deserves better than that. I just can't guarantee that things will change quickly, or at all.

Worry over my dad's presence fills me as I pull into the driveway. Luckily, his truck is gone. He'll probably stumble in close to dawn reeking of booze, and I'll have to clean up after him like I always do. If Mom never left, I wouldn't be dealing with this right now. We'd be a happy, normal family. At least, that's what I've always envisioned.

Grabbing my phone, I text Amelia to let her know I made it home. She doesn't respond, most likely asleep after spending a day in the sun. The door creaks as I open then close it behind me. The house is silent, and I soak it in because there's likely to be another fight in the coming days.

Lying in my bed, I mentally go over everything I'll need to do tomorrow and what the morning has in store for me. Thoughts of Amelia drift through my mind. A smile forms on my lips, and then quickly fades. She shouldn't be exposed to the life I lead. I tried my best to keep it all separate from her, but I'm not sure that's possibly anymore. Not now that my dad has seen her, and is set on being a dick about my relationship. Only time will tell if she sticks around. My father's voice rings through my head. "She's going to leave you just like your mom." The fear of that happening is real, and most likely going to happen. There's no way in hell she'll want to stick around for the messy parts of my life.

Trying to no longer dwell on it, I turn over and pull the blankets up around me. It's hot, yet I need the false sense of comfort being wrapped up brings.

amelia

"IS Randall coming to the party today?" Aunt Lucia asks while making yet another batch of brownies. How many sweets does she think we need? We aren't feeding an army, or at least I don't think so.

"He said he was," I reply. That was last weekend. He hasn't talked to me much this week, which is odd. Even when we can't see each other due to our work schedules, we usually keep up a pretty consistent text conversation. Or at least call each other. It hasn't been radio silence, but it might as well be. He still sends me funny memes, or ridiculous gifs, but as far as actual conversation... He's backed off quite a bit.

Did I do something last weekend to make him mad? This boyfriend terrain is so hard to navigate. Last time, I was completely blindsided by the guy I fell for. Is that happening again? Maybe he didn't like my opinion on him staying at his house. Normally, I'm not quite so brazen with my thoughts. I finally feel comfortable enough with Randall that I no longer feel I need to filter them.

"What's the matter, Amelia?" The oven door opens, and I'm sure she's putting the brownies in to cook. Unless she had a secret batch already in there, and is taking them out. I didn't smell any chocolate when I came into the kitchen, though.

"Why are boys so confusing?" I groan, and lay my head on the kitchen table. The urge to bang my head against it a few times is there, but I don't do it. That wouldn't make the jumbled thoughts in my head suddenly form something intelligible. And, it would just give me a headache, or worse, a bruise on my forehead from the frustration.

The chair beside me is pulled back from the table, and she sits down. "I take it this has something to do with Randall."

"Everything was going great. We have a real connection. One I've never felt before." Sitting up, I face my aunt. "Last weekend I saw him and his dad get in a fight, and his dad said some pretty shitty things. We talked a bit when he drove me home from the lake, since then... he hasn't been talking to me as much, and I can't help but wonder if I did something that may have upset him."

"Mija," Lucia grabs my hand. "That boy has lived a hard life. I'm sure you didn't do anything intentionally. He's probably scared of change. Anything, especially if it's different from his normal, is going to be terrifying.

Even if it's something good. Give him time, he'll come around." She gets back up from the chair. "I need to make a few more desserts for tonight."

"Are you trying to send us all to the dentist?" I laugh. "Why are you making so many sweet things? It's not like there are going to be a ton of people here."

"I know that. Some of those people will be guys, who eat a lot, though," she nods like that explains everything. "Trust me. These kids have been cleaning me out of food since they were little. It's good to be over prepared for their appetites."

Rolling my eyes, I stand. Being in this house isn't doing anything for my mood. It may be hot as hell outside, but anything is better than staying inside and dwelling on my thoughts. "If you say so. Is Uncle Jason outside?"

"Yeah, he's getting the grill ready." She gives me a knowing look, and grins. "Go do something productive. It'll help you keep your mind off things until you get a chance to see your boyfriend today."

I practically run away from the sickly-sweet smell of the kitchen. Sliding the back door open, I'm hit with another aroma. Wood being burned in the grill. It's one of the things I love about my uncle's grilling skills. He doesn't use a gas grill despite the ease of it.

Following my nose, I find Uncle Jason bringing more wood over to the grill for when he runs out. "Do you need any help?"

Small wood logs slip from his hands, and land on his

foot. "Son of a bitch, that hurts." He turns toward me. "You scared the hell out of me. I thought your cousin was the only one capable of sneaking up on people. Maybe I should put a bell around the two of you so you can't creep up on me."

"Someone has jokes today," I laugh. "And I can tell you right now exactly how Tonya would feel about you putting a bell on her."

"It definitely wouldn't go over very well." He picks the wood off the ground and stacks them neatly next to the grill. "Did you say you were looking for something to do?"

"Oh," I say. "Um, yeah. I wanted to see if you needed help with anything for the party."

"Running away from your thoughts?" He chuckles.

"How did you -" I begin asking but he cuts me off.

"You and Tonya are so much alike it's unreal. The only time I've ever seen Tonya actively look for something to do is when she's trying to get out of her head." When he sees the fear play across my face, because I'm not talking about Randall to my uncle, he continues. "Don't worry, I'm not going to ask. I trust that you'll do whatever you think is best in the end."

"So, what do you need me to do?" I bounce on my toes, ready to use some of the pent-up energy on something productive.

"Why don't you grab the extra tables and chairs from the garage, and get them set up? Not too close to the fence, or nobody will be able to see the fireworks."

I give him a smartass salute, and head to the garage. Everything is neatly put away, but there is no rhyme or reason to where items are placed. The chairs are lined up on one side of the wall behind bicycles that I've never seen them ride, and the tables are shoved behind plastic totes on the opposite side. You would think they'd have both of these things in the same vicinity since they have so many barbeques and get-togethers.

Lucky for me, the cars aren't parked in here right now. I grab all the chairs and stack them in the middle of the floor and put the tables next to them. Grabbing three chairs in each hand, I attempt to walk to the garage door, and two of them clatter to the ground when I turn. This is going to take more trips than I originally thought. Oh well, at least it'll keep me busy for a little while longer.

Once I finally have everything outside, I begin setting everything up. They are kind of close together with enough space to walk between, even if people have their chairs scooted all the way out. Uncle Jason strides over to check on my progress. "Do you need any help?"

"Nope," I shake my head. "This is the last one." Unfolding the chair, I have in my hand, I set it down with more force than necessary and collapse into it. "Why do y'all have those bikes? I've never once seen you, or Aunt Lucia, ride them."

He grabs one of the chairs, and takes a seat. "Your aunt has it in her head that one day we'll do a triathlon." He shakes his head. "I doubt that it will ever happen, but she wants to hang on to them 'just in case'" He does his fingers in air quotes.

"That seems like a pretty silly reason to keep them."

"It is," he snorts. "We keep them anyway because it makes Lucia happy. And you know the saying, happy wife, happy life? I stick to that every day."

I think about seeing them together throughout my life, and I've never once seen them fight. It happens, I know that because there's not a couple around that doesn't have some sort of disagreement. They've always seemed genuinely happy whether they are together or apart from each other. "How do you make it all work?"

"Communication, Melly," he leans back in his chair. "That's the key to everything you do in life. Whether it's relationships, jobs, or friendships, communication is what is going to keep everything on an even keel."

If that doesn't hit the nail on the head, I don't know what else will. It's the very thing I was thinking about before I came outside. The lack of real, *honest*, communication is what is bugging me. If things with Randall were carrying on like the weeks, even days before, I wouldn't be such a confused mess right now.

"It looks like you just had a lightbulb moment," Jason says into the silence.

"Maybe," I stand up, almost knocking the chair backward. "I'm going to go get ready before people start showing up."

"That sounds like a good idea. I need to get the meat on the grill."

"See you in a few," I make my way toward the house.

"While you're in there, will you tell Lucia to cool it with the desserts," he laughs. "She's going to force me to go on a diet if she doesn't stop baking."

"I'll try," I sing-song. "There's no guarantee that she'll actually listen."

* * *

"Girl, how long does it take you to get ready?" Tonya barges into what used to be her room. "Mom said you've been in here for over an hour."

"Well, first I took a shower after setting up the tables in the yard," I point at the towel hanging on the door. "Then I took a much needed nap." Sitting up from my bed, I glare at her, "Which *you* so unkindly woke me up from."

"People are starting to show up so you better get dressed," she sticks her tongue out at me. "What time is Randall supposed to be here?"

"I don't know," I shrug. "He hasn't replied to my text messages."

Her eyes widen and her mouth drops open. "Are you serious? I thought things were okay after the b.s. with his dad."

"Guess not," I pull my clothes off my bed. Walking to the bathroom, I don't bother closing the door before I start getting dressed. "I mean, we've been talking, but it's not like we were. Does that make sense?"

"Yep, and it proves my point that the male species is a pain in the ass." She leans against the bathroom door, and watches me as I put my hair into a messy bun. It's way too hot to have it down if I'm going to be outside most of the time. "Do you think he'll show up?"

"Only time will tell, cuz," sighing, I turn toward her. "It just sucks because I was considering staying here, and going to school for business management to open my own boutique one day. Now... I don't know if I should stay."

"Do *not* let a guy dictate your actions," she scolds me. "If you want to stay here, you are more than welcome. It's not like you're a drain on resources. Mom told me you've been sneaking money into her purse for rent."

"It's the only way she'll take it. The first time I tried giving it to her, she threw it back at me, and said she wasn't going to allow me to pay her anything."

"That sounds about right," Tonya rolls her eyes. "Seriously, we love having you here. It's like reliving our childhood summers, but you know, as adults."

"True," I agree. She has a point, and honestly, I don't want to leave. My parents will completely understand if I decide to stay. "I'll probably stay. It would just suck having to avoid the one person I've fallen for. It's not like this town is huge."

"It's easier to avoid people than you think," she throws her arm over my shoulders. "Trust me, I speak from experience."

"I'll take your word for it," I laugh. "Let's get out

there before your mom starts searching for us." Bumping my hip against hers, we start walking out of the room. "And when Randall shows up, I fully intend on pulling him aside to have a talk with him."

* * *

The sky is darkening, and the party is in full swing. Reaf and Jake are taking turns helping Layla play with the sparklers. It's kind of cute how they both work together to make Layla's life as normal as possible. I never would have thought it would be possible for exes to be friends, but Jake and Tonya are the epitome of a well-functioning co-parenting duo. It may have taken Jake a bit longer to jump on board, it's working well now that they are all on the same page.

The fireworks over the lake are about to start, and Randall still isn't here yet. He told me he was on his way an hour ago. The evasion and lack of talking are really starting to piss me off. I'm not a needy person, at least I don't think I am. It's not like I want us together at the hip all the time. We had an awesome groove going, and since last weekend, it's all gone awry.

Fireworks light up the sky, and Layla starts clapping in excitement. Seeing the joy on her face over something so simple as fireworks, makes me so happy. That girl may be spoiled rotten, but she knows how to enjoy the little things. Jake and Charleigh are sitting in lawn chairs beside the hammock Reaf and Tonya are occupying. Uncle Jason and Aunt Lucia are watching from their comfortable chairs on the porch. Cami, Travis, Darcy, and Derrick are sitting around the fire pit roasting marshmallows talking about how awesome the basketball season is going to be at Hilltown University. Marshall and Bianca are around here somewhere, but Bianca isn't really a people person. There are a few work colleagues my aunt and uncle invited, and I have no clue who they are or what they do.

All I know is that I'm alone at this party. Everyone is coupled up, and I'm left being the odd man out because my boyfriend has yet to make an appearance. Oh well, I guess he had more important things to do. Or, his dad started acting like a complete ass again.

The fireworks are getting bigger and coming faster, signaling the display coming to a close. I feel a pair of arms wrap around me. "I made it."

Normally, the sound of his voice would bring me joy. Right now... it grates on my nerves. "You were supposed to be here hours ago. Where have you been?" I turn around and see regret in his eyes.

"Sorry," he winces. "I got tied up with my dad."

Instead of arguing with him in front of everyone, I pull him to the side of the house. "You could have let me know. I've been wondering where you were, and worried."

"I didn't think to let you know what was going on," he reaches for my hand but I pull it away. Hurt flashes behind his eyes. "It was another rough night, and I'm here now."

"That's not good enough, Randall," I shout. Lowering my voice, I continue, "You've hardly talked to me all week. I understand you get busy, and I know you have other things you need to take care of. Damn it, we're supposed to be a couple, and I have no clue what's been going on with you. Things haven't been the same since last weekend."

"Why can't you see that I'm trying?" He whispers loudly.

"That's the thing, though." I take a step back and away from him. "You're not trying. You say you want better for your life, but you don't take any actions toward what you want. Do you think it was easy for me to move here, a place I don't know all that well, and try to rebuild my confidence? It wasn't. And yet, here I am. Doing what I need to do to make things better for myself."

"That's not fair," he argues.

"Maybe not," I say. "At the same time, how is you pushing me away when things get hard fair to me?" Silence is the only thing I'm met with, and it breaks my heart. Our friends and family celebrating behind us, and people shooting off fireworks are soundtrack to our conversation. "I've always been considerate of what you're going through. Never pushed or tried to make you choose me over your dad because that's not something I would ever do. But the lack of communication is something I can't deal with, especially if we're going all in with each other. I'm pretty sure I'm in love with you, Randall, and I want better for you. For *us*."

Randall stands staring at me. The light hanging off the roof flickers, and I can't tell what he's feeling. Not that I'd be able to if he doesn't want me know. He's great at schooling his features to hide his pain. "So, is that it then?" His tone is cool with a touch of anger.

He didn't even react when I said the "L" word. I must be the only one that feels it, and it's such a slap in the face. I opened up to him, told him my fears, as well as my hopes and dreams. "I guess so." I don't wait for him to say anything else. Walking to the back door, I slip inside without anyone else noticing. Once I'm in my bedroom, I close and lock the door before lying on the bed. My face is buried in my pillows to quiet the sounds of my sobs and heart shattering into a million pieces once again.

Tonight could have turned out differently if he had just said *something*. Instead, he stood there like what I said didn't matter. As if, I didn't matter.

randall

SHE BROKE UP WITH ME. I can't fucking believe it. Because I had other shit going on, she called things off. It's not my fault my dad's an incapable asshole. Or, that I have to take care of him so he doesn't do anything to hurt himself.

Three days should be enough time to get over being dumped, except when it's not. It's all I can think about. Even Tony has commented on my less than stellar work performance because all that keeps going through my head is her saying "I guess," and walking off without a backward glance. Maybe I didn't mean as much to her and she did to me. Maybe I've royally screwed things up.

A text message comes in, and I debate ignoring it like I have all the others. We aren't supposed to have our phones with us when we're on the floor working but I keep it on me on the off chance Amelia calls me. Pulling it out of my pocket, I check the screen, and my shoulders sag. It's only Marshall. Instead of reading it, I shove the phone back into my pocket and continue restocking the mulch.

"Hey, Randall," Tony calls from down the aisle. "Can you come here for a minute?"

Damn it. What did I do this time? Now is not a good time for me to be getting in trouble at work. I can't afford to lose this job. Back when I first started my job hunt at sixteen, Tony was the only person willing to offer me a job despite my dad's history. Most people assumed the apple didn't fall too far from the tree. But, I'm nothing like my dad. I've done everything in my power to be the complete opposite. Just because he can't seem to do hold down a job, doesn't mean I'm the same way.

"Yeah, sure thing," I throw my gloves on the pallet that still needs to be unloaded. "What's up?"

"Look," he hooks his thumbs through his belt loops. "I'm not usually one to meddle in the lives of my employees." When I raise an eyebrow in rebuttal, he adds, "much." This is starting to sound like a lecture. "Is everything okay? Last week you seemed off, but this week... It's like your whole personality has changed. You just seem really angry. Did your dad say, or *do*, anything to you?"

Has my attitude really shown that much at work? Keeping my personal life separate from my work life is something I've always been really good at. That is, until Amelia caught my eye.

When I don't answer, he says, "I'm really not trying

to intrude. I only want what's best for you, and to see you succeed. You've been happy, and close to giddy, for a while. And to see you reverting back to that troubled teenager I hired all those years ago is worrisome."

"Why does everyone keep saying they want what's best for me?" I retort. It's loud enough that a few customers walking around the corner, turn to see what's going on.

Tony doesn't miss the curious glances. "Let's go to my office and talk." When I open my mouth to protest, he puts his hands up in surrender. "You're not going to be fired, Randall. You *need* to talk to someone. And if I can be that person, I'll feel better."

Even though he says he's not going to fire me, if I don't at least appease him, he'll send me home. Causing me to lose precious hours that I desperately need. "Okay, let's go talk."

Following him through the store to his office, I do my best to keep my head down. My coworkers are peeking up from what they are doing to see what's going, but I look in the opposite direction when I happen to make eye contact with them. Great. Now there will be whispers about me going around the store. Maybe I do need an attitude adjustment. Right now, though, I feel like I can't function. The hole Amelia ripped in my heart is jagged, and hurts so fucking much I can hardly breathe.

Once we're safely tucked away in the office, Tony closes and locks the door. Not only to keep prying ears from listening in, but so that we aren't interrupted either. A small part of me hopes there is some sort of customer emergency that needs his approval so I don't have to talk about my feelings. It doesn't happen, though. He takes a seat behind his desk, and motions for me to sit in the chair opposite him.

"We're away from everyone else, now." He leans forward. "You've always been like a son to me, and I'll help you with whatever you need." At my nod, he continues, "Is this about that girl you've been so smitten with, or your father?"

Who the hell says smitten anymore? It's like he's stuck in some fifties after school special. If I don't answer, he'll wait me out. He's always been really good at that. "Both," I shrug.

"Well, why don't you start at the beginning?" He grabs his bottle of water, and sets it in front of him. Patiently waiting for me to speak.

The office is getting hot, and I can feel my heartbeat racing. It reminds me of when I would get sent to the principal's office in school. Though I'm not in any sort of trouble here. Well, not legally, anyway. My emotions are the threat and I'm not sure I can handle it.

"My dad and I got into it again the weekend before last, and Amelia witnessed it all." My fingers tap an unsteady rhythm against my leg. "He said some things about her, and I might have started to believe them."

"Like what," he asks, brows furrowed.

"He said she would leave me just like my mom left us. I really like this girl. Honestly, I'm pretty sure I love her. As much as I tried to shrug his comments off, I began dwelling on them." My right-hand clenches at the thought of how he treated us that day. How he treated *her*, as if she didn't exist and was inconsequential. "I pulled away. We would text all the time, and I stopped doing that as much. I would stay busy."

Tony interrupts me, "Is that why you picked up the extra shifts last week?" I nod. "Okay, go on."

This feels like I'm sitting in a therapist's office. All we're missing is the couch for me to lie on. I'm used to this kind of questioning. After my mom bailed, and I began acting out in class, my teacher suggested I speak with the school's guidance counselor. In the end, I told her what she wanted to hear, not what I was actually feeling. I don't want to do that with Tony. He's one of the few good role models I have, and it would be a disservice to him, me, and Amelia. The only way to move on is to get it all out.

"When I showed up late, after my shift here, for the Fourth of July party, she confronted me about blowing her off. She laid out all of her feelings and hopes for us. But I didn't say anything." Burying my face in my hands, I groan. I'm a fucking idiot. "She said she was falling in love with me, and I repaid her by getting pissed off and daring her to break up with me."

"And that's the reason for your foul mood this week," Tony claps. "So, what are you going to do about it?"

"There's nothing left to do," I lean back in my chair until I'm staring at the ceiling. "She hasn't reached out to me, and I'm pretty sure she'll go back to her hometown now that I've royally screwed things up."

"Or...," he begins. "You can man up, admit you were a dumbass, and win your girl back."

"It's not as easy as you make it sound, old man."

He chuckles, "I never said it would be easy. Anything worth fighting for takes work." Clasping his hands on the desk, he leans forward. "First, you need to get your life in order."

"What do you mean?" I'm playing dumb. I know exactly what he means. His words will help solidify it, though. They'll give me the push I've been too scared to make. Even when it meant losing Amelia.

"You need to get out of that house." He stares at me, waiting for me to argue. "I know he's your dad, but he is an *adult* and perfectly capable of taking care of himself. He's taking advantage of you. Preying off your guilt."

"You think I don't know that?" I huff and cross my arms over my chest. "I've wanted to leave so many times. He shut down and started drinking when Mom bailed on us. What do you think he's going to do when I leave?"

"You can't base what you're going to do on what he might do. It's not fair to you."

"Yeah, I know. It just worries me," I say in defeat.

"For now, you need to focus on you. This can't be the job you want for the rest of your life. You should be out there living your life, not worrying about others' lack of decision making skills."

"Thanks, Tony." I stand up. "I'm going to get back to

work now. Looks like I have a lot of butt kissing and planning to do."

"Good," he nods. "I'm glad I finally got through to you. If you need help finding a place to stay, let me know."

"Will do." Not waiting for him to say anything else, I walk out of his office. He's right, and I've chosen not to do anything about my life. Coasting through and hoping everything is going to magically get better isn't doing me any favors. It's time to make some hard decisions.

amelia

DRIVING through town brings on so many memories. Some bad, but most are good. I didn't think I'd be home so soon. *Home* doesn't really describe this place anymore though, not since I've been living in Asheville. It took me getting my heart broken for me to find myself, make some amazing new friends, and figure out what I want to do with my life.

Mom and Dad are standing on the front porch when I pull into the driveway. How long have they been out here? It's hotter here than it was in Asheville, and I never let them know what time I was going to be in.

"Oh, Mija," Mom is hustling to my car before I even have the door all the way open. "I've missed you so much."

Before I have a chance to respond, she pulls me out of the car and wraps her arms around me in a tight embrace. As much Aunt Lucia's hugs help when I need them, there's nothing like being in my mom's arms. All of my worries disappear, at least for the moment. "I missed you to, Mom."

"How is everyone? How's Layla?" She asks, guiding me toward the porch. Dad's covering his mouth with his hand, trying to hold in his laughter.

"Woah," I laugh. "Slow down. I'll be here all week. Let me say hi to Dad before you pepper me with questions."

Rolling her eyes, she walks into the house. I throw my arms around my dad and squeeze. "Hi, Daddy. It feels like it's been forever."

"It hasn't been that long," he pats my head the way he used to when I was little. "We're happy to have you home."

"I'm happy to be home."

He pulls back, eyebrows scrunched together. "Really? I figured this is the last place you'd want to be after... Well, after that *boy* got to you."

Dad was never Andrew's biggest fan. Whenever he would come over for dinner, or hang out, Dad would act like he didn't exist. I should have known then that Andrew was bad news.

"I'm good," I nod. "My job back in Asheville is going great and Aunt Lucia helped me register for school in the fall."

"I thought you didn't want to do the whole college thing?"

Shrugging, I open the door to go inside the house. "If

I'm going to own my own boutique store one day, I figure I need at least take some business classes so I can get started on the right foot."

"I'm so proud of you, Mijita." He closes the door behind us, blocking out the stifling heat. "I think your mama was hoping you'd change your mind and stay, but she'll be happy for you, too."

"It's not like our family doesn't get together at every possible opportunity," I snort. "I'm sure you'll still see me pretty often. Did you happen to get some boxes for me?"

"They're in your room. You're not going to start packing right now are you?"

I shake my head. "Nope. I'm going to annoy you and Mom as much as I can before I start in on it. I'm sure it'll take me most of the week to go through everything."

"Come eat," Mom yells from the kitchen.

"This is why I keep gaining weight," he pats his stomach. "Your mom won't stop making food. I think it's how she copes."

"It must run in the family because Lucia is *always* baking. It's weird."

Following Dad into the kitchen, I take a seat at the kitchen table I've eaten so many meals at. It feels good to be home, listening to my parents bicker over ridiculous things, and feeling more like myself than I ever have before.

* * *

Everything at my old job is the same. There's a teenager working behind the counter for the summer. She smiles as I walk into the store. "Hi, let me know if you need help with anything."

"I will." She reminds me of myself. Well, the me that existed before Andrew destroyed me and Randall helped put me back together. Only to ruin me even more. Falling in love wasn't something I had in mind when I moved to Asheville. My plan was to be the surly girl that sticks to herself. Except the brown eyed guy that was a jackass as a kid reeled me in. Making me care about him, then shutting down when things got tough. One day it won't hurt anymore. For now, I'll wear that pain like a badge of honor. Connecting with him gave me the courage to figure out what I truly want. It'd be better if he was a part of it, but I'm not going to force him.

"Amelia, is that you?" I whip around at my name. Sheila, my former boss, is standing outside the dressing room with a grin on her face. "I was wondering when I'd see you again. Are you here to work again?"

"It's so good to see you," I give her a quick hug. "I'm only in town for the week packing some things to take back to Asheville with me."

"Bummer," she frowns. "I was hoping you were here to stay."

"You aren't the only one." A cute flowery dress catches my eye. The top looks as if it hugs your body, and the skirt flares out a bit. It reminds of something Bianca would wear, only softer. Mentally calculating how much money I have, I pull it down from the display.

"Your mom and I can dream," she sighs. "Were you looking for anything in particular?"

"No, I just wanted to come by to see you, and see how the shop is holding up without me."

"I'd be lying if I said I wasn't a mess for a little bit. Things are under control now." She reaches for the dress in my hands. "Here, let me set that at the counter so you don't have to carry it while you look around."

"Thanks." A headband with a big bow catches my eye, and I know I *have* to get it for Layla. She hates them with a passion and always pulls them off, but she'll look adorable for the whole two seconds she'll wear it.

Grabbing it, I take it to the counter. If I don't buy my items now, I'll spend all my money in this store. It was one of the hazards of me working here. My checks almost always went right back to the store.

"Give her the employee discount, Julie." How in the world did she know I was about to pay? I don't bother arguing with her. It's pointless. Sometimes I think Sheila went into the wrong career. She'd make one hell of a lawyer with her talent in arguments.

"Thank you, Sheila," I yell loud enough for her to hear me in the back room.

"You're welcome, Hon. Don't be a stranger."

I'm almost to my car when I hear *his* voice. "Hey there, hotness. Long time no see." His group of friends, my friends for a short period of time, snicker behind him.

"What do you want, Andrew?" My voice is clipped. Clearly, I'm not in the mood to deal with him. I knew there was a chance I'd run into him while here. I just didn't think it would happen within twenty-four hours of me being back.

"Ah," he sneers. "You didn't miss me?"

Part of me wants to shrink inside myself and hide from the asshole. Instead, I'm going to channel my inner Cami and not take any shit from him. "You didn't even cross my mind." It's a lie, and he doesn't need to know that.

"I don't believe that." He sticks his chest out like he's some sort of rooster trying to prove he's the top bird. He looks ridiculous, and I don't know why I fell for his charm in the first place.

"Believe what you want," I wave him off in dismissal. "I've got things to do."

He opens his mouth to say something else, but I don't hear it. Getting in my car, I put the key in the ignition and start it. The air conditioner is running at full capacity, and I want nothing more than to be riding around with Randall in his car with the windows down.

I may put on an even keeled facade. It's just that, though, fake. My heart wants the one person I walked away from.

randall

EVERYTHING IS in place for me to win Amelia back. With a good word from Jake and Tony, I now have an apartment. It also happens to be in the same complex Tonya and Reaf live in. I really hope my plan works well or things could get awkward. It's a good thing I live on the opposite side of the complex from them, just in case.

Standing in the middle of my new living room, it feels lonely. I don't have any furniture yet. The only room that has anything in it is my bedroom because it's filled with all the things that came from my father's house. Buying new to me furnishings is on my list of things I need to take care of, but it's not the most pressing item. That spot belongs to one person alone... Amelia. Hopefully she'll give me a chance to say what I need to before slamming a door in my face.

Keys in hand, I walk out of the front door and lock it

behind me. My steps are slow. As excited as I am about seeing Amelia, I'm also nervous and scared. It may be too late for me to salvage the mess I made by not speaking up. First on my agenda is flowers. According to Jake, they help when you're trying to get in your girl's good graces. The hard part will be choosing the perfect flower for her. One thing is for sure, roses are out. They don't fit her personality, and the only way I'm going to wow her is if I put some thought into my selection. It's not a lot. At least it's a small gesture to show her I'm in it for the long haul. I'm just happy she enjoys the little things and doesn't need me to make a big scene. Otherwise, I'd be screwed.

Amelia's car isn't parked at the curb, or in the driveway, when I pull up to her house. I'm equal parts dismayed and relieved. If she's not here, I don't have to feel like a complete dumbass when she rejects me. Fear urges me to turn around and go back home. I'm tired of living a life where I'm scared to fall for someone so completely, I give them the ability to hurt me. Or worse... leave me. Amelia already did that, and yet here I am. Not able to let her go.

Pushing aside my doubts, I grab the daisies I bought her and step out of the car. One foot in front of the other, that's the only way I'm going to know I gave *us* my best shot.

The air outside of my car is cooler than it was inside.

Fixing the air conditioner is another top priority. Or, maybe I'm freaking out. Patting my face with my hands, I check to see if I have sweat dripping down my face. When my hands come away dry, I breathe a sigh of relief. There's nothing worse than showing up to impress someone when you look sweaty and gross.

My heart drums a rapid beat as I advance toward the front door. Feet moving at a slow pace while I try to figure out exactly what I'm going to say. I didn't think this part through. Maybe I should have so I don't look like a complete moron.

The door is a mere five feet away. Three feet. One foot. All I have to do is knock. The flowers in my hand are starting to wilt, and I debate hiding them around the corner. They look like such a sad offering now that I'm here. I inhale deeply, then exhale. Raising my closed hand, I knock on the door three times. Tap. Tap. Tap.

A minute passes. Then two minutes. It doesn't seem like anyone is home, which is a possibility since I didn't see any of their cars in the driveway. Now the sweat starts beading on my forehead. It's never taken them this long to answer the door. Do I wait, or go? If I leave it will botch the entire gesture. Another two minutes go by and my forehead isn't the only thing sweating. My shirt is beginning to stick to me and it's uncomfortable. I can't come to her looking like a mess.

The decision is taken out of my hands. As I'm turning to leave, the front door opens. I whip around expecting to see Amelia, but it's Mrs. Burgess. She doesn't not look happy to see me. "Did you need something, Randall?"

This is not something I accounted for. Which is stupid because she lives with them. Of course, there was a chance somebody besides Amelia would answer the door. "Um," I shuffle my feet and stare at the ground. "Is Amelia home?"

"No," she says, matter of fact. "She went home."

"What? When?" There are so many more questions I want to ask, but those feel like the most important.

"A couple of days ago. Did you want me to give her a message?"

She went home? For good? As much as I want to say this out loud, I don't. It won't do me any good. Not right now, at least. "No, that's okay." Lifting the flowers up to her, I urge her to take them. "These were supposed to be for Amelia." She stares at the drooping flowers for a second before taking them. "Sorry, the heat kind of messed them up. Sorry for taking up your time."

My back is to the door, and Mrs. Burgess, in two seconds flat. That was embarrassing. "I'll tell her you stopped by," she calls to my retreating back. I really hope she doesn't. This whole excursion was pitiful. I need a better plan because I am not giving up.

* * *

Twenty minutes later, I'm knocking on Tonya's front door. A sneaking suspicion tells me she's not going to be as nice as her mom was. Not that Mrs. Burgess was all warm hugs and smiles. I'm not disappointed when she swings the door open, glaring at me. "What do you want, Randall?"

"I need Amelia's address." There's no point in beating around the bush. She'll either give it to me, or she won't. It's that simple.

"Why should I give it to you?" She crosses her arms over her chest, daring me to give her a good reason.

"I need to tell her how I feel. She wasn't," I don't get a chance to finish because Tonya interrupts me.

"You had a chance to tell her how you felt. And you stood there like a dumbass and let her walk away from you."

"I know," I groan. "I freaked out. You know my history, how my mom left us, and the shit I dealt with on a daily basis with my dad."

"What do you mean dealt?" She takes a step back, trying to see if she can figure out what changed by my appearance alone. This is not her brightest moment, but I'm sure as shit not telling her that. She's the only person standing between me and Amelia. It wouldn't be wise to insult her right now.

"Can I come in?" I point inside. "It's a little toasty out here."

"Yes," she points at me. "I want answers. Especially if you want me to help you with Amelia."

"Understood."

She opens the door wider to allow me entrance. The cold air conditioning feels like heaven compared to standing on her porch. Honestly, I'm surprised she gave in so easily. That *has* to mean something.

Once I'm seated on her couch, she stares me down. "So, what did you mean dealt with? Aren't you still living with your dad?"

Shaking my head, I lean back and get comfortable. "Tony and Jake helped me get an apartment. In this complex, actually." I sweep my hands in front of me to clarify my point. "I'm on the other side, but I have my own place now."

"What made you decide to move out?"

"Tony sat me down and talked to me," I shrug. "He hit me with some hard truths, and helped me realize some things. Including how much I love your cousin."

"Jake and Marshall have only been trying to do that for years," she mutters, not realizing I can hear her. "So, you do feel the same way," she says a bit louder. It's not a question and I can't help the small cry of victory in my head. There's still a chance.

"Yep. I have for a while," I pause. "And that's why I need your help. I went to your parents' house and your mom said Amelia went home. Is she staying there for good?"

"No, she's just going to get some of her things and spend time with her mom and dad."

"Any chance you're going to give me her address?" I

smile and wag my eyebrows hoping she finds some sympathy for me and just tells me already.

"Promise to never hurt her again?"

"I'll do everything in my power to ensure she's happy." She opens her mouth as if to argue, except I don't give her a chance. "It won't always be easy, but *she's* worth fighting for."

A smile creeps over her face. "That is exactly the answer I was hoping for." She glances at me and winces. "I'm going to give you her address. It's a long drive, and no offense, but your car probably won't make it that far and back."

"Shit." Not exactly what I wanted to hear. I'll figure something out. Marshall or Jake will most likely let me borrow one of their cars. "Okay."

"I have an idea," she taps her fingers together like some sort of villainous overlord.

"Which is..." She's making me antsy with all the long pauses and taking forever to answer a simple question.

She sits on the opposite side of the couch from me. "I'm going to come with you, and we'll take my car."

"What about Layla?" It's odd that she's so gung-ho about a road trip with me.

"I'll ask my mom if she'll keep her for a couple of days, and see if Reaf can take off work to join us. Though I'm sure he won't have a problem with it if he can't."

"Okay," I drawl. "But what's your reasoning for going?"

"I haven't seen my aunt and uncle since the wedding," she shrugs. "And I'm sure she's going to need more than just her car to haul her crap back here. She didn't listen to me when I offered to take my car down there, too."

"Basically, you just want to prove a point and get your way," I shake my head.

"Exactly," she grins. "We'll leave tomorrow morning."

"Sounds like a plan." I stand up, and I'm not sure if I should hug her or shake her hand. This is something I never would have expected, least of all from her.

"I'll call you if anything changes."

"Thank you," I breathe out. "You have no idea how much this means to me. And if she rejects me, at least I can say I tried."

"You've grown up a lot, Randall," she studies me as if I'm some unknown object. "Adulting suits you."

"Whatever," I roll my eyes. "I guess I'll see you bright and early."

"Yep."

It's starting to get awkward, so I head toward the door. What kind of parallel universe is this that the girl I once had a crush on is the one helping me fix things with her cousin.

As soon as I'm outside, I text Tony letting him know I'm finally going to cash in on my vacation days and need the next few days off. His response is quick.

· · ·

Tony: We'll get your shifts covered. Good luck with your girl.
Randall: Thanks. I have a feeling I'm going to need it.

The drive from Tonya's apartment to mine takes two minutes, but I'm already mentally going over everything I need to get together. This is my second, okay maybe third, chance and I'm not going to blow it.

amelia

BOXES LITTER MY ROOM. There's one big box that I've been filling up to donate to a local shelter. Anything I'm not taking back to Asheville with me gets tossed in there. Leaving them in this room to collect dust is ridiculous. I only wish I had realized just how much crap I've accumulated over the years. Maybe now is a good time to donate everything, and start over. A fresh new me to begin my new adventure.

"Amelia," Mom calls from somewhere in the house. If I was a betting woman, I would say the kitchen. She's been cooking up a storm since I've been home. It's like she thinks Aunt Lucia doesn't feed me. "Come eat something. You've been in there all day and you need a break."

Looks like I was right. If she keeps feeding me, I'm going to have to start working out. Well, I should be doing that anyway, but it's not number one on the list of things I enjoy doing. "I'll be there in a minute," I holler.

My stomach growls in protest. Clearly not happy that I haven't followed the scent of arroz con pollo to the kitchen. I guess, I'm going now. Throwing the shirt in my hand toward the donation box, I stand up and stretch my cramped muscles. How long was I sitting there? It had to have been at least a couple of hours because the massive pile of clothes at the foot of my bed had dwindled down to a small stack. All I know is I'm making progress.

My bedroom floor has turned into an obstacle course, and I hop over piles until I'm at the door. The boxes I'm taking with me are labeled and neatly stacked against the wall. There's no way all of this is going to fit in my car. I'll either have to make two trips, or mom will have to bring some with her the next time she comes to visit. Tonya was right about needing two cars, but I'll never tell her that. She would bring it up every chance she got.

No longer able to resist the aroma coming from the kitchen, I join my mom. There's already a plate, with homemade tortillas beside it, waiting for me at the table. She spoils me, and I've missed it while being at my aunt and uncle's.

"How's the packing going?" She sits down in the chair opposite me.

"Why did you let me get so much stuff?" I whine. "I feel like I'm never going to get through it all before I have to go back."

"Or you could stay," she says quietly.

"You know I can't, Mom," I sigh. "I have a job to get

back to, and I'm doing really well in Asheville. I have friends and I'm starting school in the fall."

"Why can't you have all that here?"

"Because all the "friends" I had here were horrible to me. It's a fresh start for me there, and I've gotten really close with some of the girls."

"Okay," she relents. "I'll stop bugging you about staying. But you don't have to pack up *everything* while you're here. It's not like you're never coming back."

She has a point. "I'll get through what I can, and at least get everything put up where it goes until I can come get more."

Nodding, she stands, and starts for the sink to wash dishes. Knocking, and Tonya's voice, stop her in her tracks. "Is that your cousin?"

I jump up, and race for the door, fork still in my hand. Throwing the door open, I see Tonya smiling broadly at me. Reaf is right next to her, and behind them is Randall. What the hell is he doing here? With them?

"I brought you a present, prima," she glances back at Randall. "And an extra car."

"How do you know if I need a car or not?" If she's going to be a Mrs. Know It All, I'm not going to let her in. Not yet, at least.

"Well, do you?" She raises one eyebrow. She must be practicing that in the mirror because she's never been able to do it before.

"Yes," I groan. "I need another car. You were right."

"I knew it," she shrieks. "One day you'll listen to me."

"I seriously doubt that," I mutter under my breath. "Come in. Y'all must be dying out there in this heat."

"We," she points between Reaf and herself, "are going to start loading up boxes. You," she puts her finger in my face. "You going to take your happy little butt out there and talk to him."

I don't need her to point out who she's talking about. It's apparent by the terrified look he has on his face. "Fine. The boxes that are going with me are stacked against the wall."

"Yes, ma'am. We'll get those loaded in both of our cars." She grabs Reaf by the hand and pulls him inside.

However, I'm left standing at the door, looking anywhere but at *him*. "Why are you here?"

"To apologize," he takes a step closer. "I also brought you these."

He whips out a bouquet of daisies from behind his back. They are fresh so they must have stopped somewhere in town. "Thank you," I whisper. "And you don't need to apologize, I know where you stand when it comes to us. You made it perfectly clear at the party."

"If I did that," he laughs, "would I have come all this way to talk to you?" He doesn't give me a chance to answer his question. He barrels ahead, "No, I wouldn't. They are here because of me. My car wouldn't make the drive, and Tonya offered to drive with me in her car."

Well if that isn't a complete one eighty, I don't know what is. When I first got involved with Randall, she warned me away from him. Now she's helping him? Traitor. "Come in, we can talk in the living room."

"Thanks." He steps around me, but close enough that his arm brushes mine and tingles replace the area he just touched.

Motioning for him to follow me into the living room, I take a deep breath. Maybe I was wrong. It's happened before, except this may be a good kind of wrong. Even though I've been angry with him, I've also missed him. Missed our daily texts and phone calls. Being wrapped up in his arms. Every single thing we did together has been on a constant loop in my mind.

He doesn't take a seat when we walk into the living room. He turns abruptly, and takes my hands in his own. "I'm so sorry. I was a moron for not speaking up when I had the chance. I love you, and I have for a while now. I was just too afraid to tell you in case you left. I let all the crap my dad said get to me. Please give me another chance to prove to you how great we are together."

Pulling away from him, I take a seat on the sofa. "And what about when he says it again, or pulls some drunken stunt? Are you going to let that get to your head, too?"

"He's not my problem anymore. I moved out."

"You, you did?" That must have been a huge step for him, leaving his dad, and dealing with his guilt.

"Yeah," he nods. "I couldn't justify staying there. Or being the parent any longer. Not when it cost me the most amazing person I know. I refuse to let it happen again."

I want nothing more than to be with Randall. He makes me want to do so much more with my life. After seeing everything he's had to handle since he was little, it gave me the courage to do what makes me happy. He's the only person, save Tonya, that I feel comfortable being myself around. Fear of being hurt again winds its way through my veins.

He's silent, waiting for me to speak. To make up my mind. Even though I'm scared, I can't let past experiences dictate how I live my life. I want to be with Randall. Through the easy and difficult times.

His shoulders sag at my lack of response. He must be feeling the same exact way I did at the party. I could let him stew in his pain a little longer, but that would make me a horrible person. Especially when being with him makes me happy. "Okay."

His head snaps up. "Okay... what?"

"I'm willing to give us another chance."

Randall pulls me up from the sofa, and twirls me around, almost knocking the lamp in the corner over. "Are you sure? I don't want you to feel pressured."

"I'm positive," I say. "On one condition."

"Anything," he agrees. "Name it and it's done."

"You can't pull away from me again. If something is bothering you, I want us to talk about it. Relationships aren't a one-way street. They require communication." I lean back the tiniest fraction. "Agreed?"

"Absolutely," he pulls me back into his arms. "This past week without talking to you has been hell. I would keep my phone on me at all times in hopes you would call me. Text me. *Something*."

"I guess it's a good thing you don't have to worry about that anymore, huh." Instead of waiting for him to kiss me, I throw my arms around his neck and lift up on my toes until my mouth meets his. I've missed kissing these lips. As soon as they touch, I feel whole. He is the piece I've been missing all along.

Mom clears her throat loud enough for us to hear, and we pull apart from each other. "So, this is the boy that broke your heart in Asheville."

"No mom," I grin. "He helped put me back together."

epilogue

THERE ARE students milling about around campus, and I don't care about any of them. Except for the one currently holding my hand. I never thought I'd get the chance to go back to school. For the longest time I had it in my head that my life would be centered around making sure Dad didn't do anything to hurt himself, or anyone else. But here I am, at Asheville Community College, doing just that.

Don't get me wrong, I still worry about my dad. He's doing better, though. He checked into rehab not long after I moved out. Determined to get his drinking under control and work through his issues concerning my mom. I'm proud of the progress he's made. At the same time, there's a voice in my head reminding me that he could fall off the wagon at any time.

"Which building are we supposed to be in?" Amelia

asks as we walk across the lawn. It's not a huge campus, but we've never been here before, and we're a little lost.

"It should be this one," I point toward the brick building directly in front of us. "I'm sure we aren't the only ones running late for Freshman orientation. I mean look at all the people hanging around the building."

My guess is they don't want to be the first ones to go in. Most of them are straight out of high school. There aren't many people our age going to this orientation. We should be close to graduating if we'd done college right out of high school. Luckily for me, a few of my classes from before carried over.

"I guess you're right," she leans into me. "Let's get in there so we can get this over with. I'm antsy enough about starting school so late in the game."

"Don't be nervous." We stop just to the left of the door. "You are going to do great. Before long you'll be able to manage that boutique single-handedly."

"If you say so," she mutters.

"I do." Those two little words remind me how we reconnected. Who would have thought I'd have a girl-friend? After years of pushing people away, I almost gave up on finding someone. But our broken pieces made each other whole, and I wouldn't trade her for anything.

Pulling her toward me, I grab her cheeks and tilt her head back. I kiss her until she's holding onto me, relying on me to keep her grounded. "You've got this, babe. We both do. We're going to shake up this town and show them what we're capable of... Together."

* * *

Prologue

Slivers of moonlight filter in through the blinds, illuminating the otherwise dark room. Dawson lies next to me, snoring softly. This is something I would have found adorable when we started dating. Now, it's annoying that he can sleep peacefully. He should be the one wide awake, in turmoil over the words he's thrown at me.

Instead, I'm the one curled up into a ball wondering how the hell I got here. It's not how I envisioned our lives together. When we first moved in together, everything was *perfect*. We spent time together every night, and I knew he adored me. Now... Now, I'm always waiting for the other shoe to drop. Never knowing when something I say is going to set him off. Every day is like walking on eggshells, hoping he'll be in a good mood.

If my parents knew how badly my relationship has gone downhill, they would be appalled. Dawson has never laid a hand on me, but the verbal slams pain me almost as much. A shard of glass, glinting in the corner, catches my eye. It's a small reminder of pissing him off earlier this evening because I didn't fold his laundry the way he likes it. The vase hitting the wall before shattering will forever be etched into my mind. I should be used to it by now, the sound of whatever he can get his hands on hitting the wall. But it's not something I should ever have to be accustomed to.

Everyone has an opinion about how they would react if they found themselves in this sort of situation. They will never truly know the fear that courses through you at the thought of leaving. The lengths a person like Dawson will go through in order to keep you by their side. The *I'm sorry's*, and empty promises. All of it grooming you, cultivating you to do what you're *supposed* to do, and stand beside them. Even when the very sight of them makes you sick to your stomach.

But no more. At least, not for me. I'm done being the person he takes out his anger on. No longer willing to be the one he uses to make himself feel big. I am better than this. I *deserve* more than this.

With one last glance at Dawson's sleeping form, I gently climb out of bed. The bags I packed hours before he got home await me in the coat closet. Most would call me a coward for taking off in the middle of the night, but it's the only time I can ensure that I'm going to get out with my dignity intact.

As quietly as possible, I pull my bags out of the closet and my keys off the key hook. Opening the door, I breathe in the cold winter night. My first taste of freedom in over six months. A voice from down the hallway stops me in my tracks.

"Going somewhere?" Dawson asks, voice scratchy with sleep.

Part of me wants to turn around and put my bags

up. To beg for forgiveness and hope this isn't the time he'll begin using his fists. But I push that reaction down, determined to take my stand and be the strong person I know is hidden deep inside me. "Yeah," my voice comes out in a squeak. Clearing my throat I try again. "Yes, I'm going to my parents."

"No, you aren't," he takes a step toward me, hands curled into fists at his side.

The urge to retreat courses through me. Dropping my bags and running for my car would be the easiest option. But... It could also end with me stumbling over something and hurting myself in the process. If I don't stand up for myself now, there's no guarantee I won't come back to him later. It's a vicious cycle, and one that I'm sick of. Straightening my back, I broaden my shoulders. I *refuse* to let him intimidate me the way he has. Refuse to let him think he can control for one second longer. "Yes, I am," I lift my chin higher. "I'm done, Dawson. This isn't working for me. The yelling, throwing things at me... I deserve more than that. You aren't the man I thought you were when we first moved in together. I won't be your prisoner anymore."

Tightening my grip on my keys in one hand, and my bag in the other, I step outside the door. This place is no longer my home. "Goodbye, Dawson."

"You can't just leave me, Sophie." His voice is pained. "I'll do better. Go to counseling. Anything." The sad thing is, I've heard all this before. Things will be great between us for a week or two, then it's back to the same old story.

"Sorry," I close the door behind me and walk briskly to my car. Fear makes me want to look back, but I don't. He's not going to follow me. Not yet, anyway. I'm sure he'll show up at my parents' house with some sob story. But by then, it'll be too late. They'll know the truth of how my life has been. There's no way Mom, or Dad, will let him come anywhere near me.

Unlocking my car door, I throw my bags into the passenger seat before sliding behind the wheel. A glance toward the apartment shows Dawson's shadowed outline in the doorway. Without taking my eyes off the door, I start the car and put it in gear. It's time to rebuild myself and put everything Dawson tore down back together.

acknowledgments

The Taking Chances series is almost finished, and I don't know if I'm excited, or sad, to be leaving these characters. But there's still one more book to go!

It truly does take a village to write a book. From my Alpha readers, who sometimes get messages at two in the morning. Melanie, Jennifer, Cindy, Cass & Carine, thank you for always going above and beyond!

My writing tribe, I'm looking at you Kelsie & Tasha... I seriously don't know what I would do without you wonderful ladies in my life. I love our daily talks, and my world is better with you in it.

My reader group is freaking awesome, and helps me with names and anything else I throw at them. I love our monthly movie nights and getting to know you all better.

My editor, Shelly Small, and cover designer, KP Designs, both of you make my books look so pretty. Thank you for everything!

I'm especially thankful for all the readers and bloggers out there that have taken a chance on me, and my books. You are the reason I do this!

Last but not least, my family & bestie. Y'all push me,

deal with my late nights, or ramblings about whatever I'm working on. Your support means everything. I love y'all to the moon and back.

The Taking Chances Series

Welcome to Your Life

Cruel and Beautiful World

Ways to Go

Remember That Night

My Only Wish is You

From This Moment

Shoot Down the Stars

Love Will Save Your Soul

Gone in Love Series

Out of the Ashes Series

Cocky Hero Club

Big Baller

Silverwood Bulldog Series

Baseball & Broadway

about the author

Katrina Marie lives in the Dallas area with her husband, two children, and fur baby. She is a lover of all things geeky and Gryffindor for life. When she's not writing you can find her at her children's sporting events, or curled up reading a book.

Visit her online: katrinamarieauthor.com

Sign up for my newsletter for extras from Welcome to Your Life: http://bit.ly/2BlDSsZ

facebook.com/KatrinaMarieAuthor

twitter.com/katrmarieauthor

instagram.com/katrinamarieauthor

amazon.com/Katrina-Marie/e/B0749SZVTK/ref=dp_byline_cont_ebooks_1

bookbub.com/profile/katrina-marie

www.ingramcontent.com/pod-product-compliance
Lightning Source LLC
Chambersburg PA
CBHW050848190726
48286CB00007B/2288